Philip Henry Wicksteed

Four Lectures on Henrik Ibsen

dealing chiefly with his metrical works

Philip Henry Wicksteed

Four Lectures on Henrik Ibsen
dealing chiefly with his metrical works

ISBN/EAN: 9783337423308

Printed in Europe, USA, Canada, Australia, Japan

Cover: Foto ©Andreas Hilbeck / pixelio.de

More available books at **www.hansebooks.com**

The Dilettante Library.

HENRIK IBSEN.

FOUR LECTURES

ON

HENRIK IBSEN

DEALING CHIEFLY WITH HIS METRICAL WORKS.

'BY

PHILIP H. WICKSTEED, M.A.

AUTHOR OF "DANTE: SIX SERMONS," "THE ALPHABET OF ECONOMIC
SCIENCE," ETC., ETC.

LONDON

SWAN SONNENSCHEIN & CO

NEW YORK: MACMILLAN & CO

1892

To

FRÖKEN VALBORG PLATOV

THESE STUDIES ARE DEDICATED

IN GRATEFUL RECOGNITION OF HER UNWEARIED ZEAL

IN HELPING ENGLISH VISITORS TO ENJOY AND TO APPRECIATE

NORWAY AND HER POETS.

PREFACE.

It is the special purpose of these Lectures (originally delivered in the Chelsea Town Hall) to call attention to a part of Ibsen's work which is still very little known in England ; and so to help towards the formation of a larger and calmer judgment of him than is at present common.

The atmosphere of controversy is hostile to a wise and fruitful appreciation ; and a "cult" is always annoying to those who do not join in it, and generally hurtful to those who do. It must surely be the desire of all, who are free from passion, to escape from the forced and unnatural polemics which seem to be an unhappy necessity laid upon us when we meet with anything to which we are not accustomed. And surely the time is not now distant when we may be allowed to admire Ibsen without striking an attitude, and may pass him by (if we do not care for him) without making a grimace.

In the hope of helping forward this consummation, I address myself particularly, though not, of course, exclusively, to that large class of readers who have themselves seen nothing specially admirable in Ibsen, but yet are not content to dismiss his admirers as the victims of a wanton caprice or a morbid love of things hateful.

I do not wish to make anyone read Ibsen who does not like him ; but I shall be glad if I can help candid readers, who have not been drawn to him, to understand, at least in part, what there is in him that attracts others.

———

The whole of the first, and a great part of the third, of these Lectures have already appeared in the "Contemporary Review," and are reprinted by the kind permission of the Editor.

The details as to Ibsen's biography are drawn entirely from H. Jaeger's book.[1]

The translations from Ibsen, in this volume, (such as they are), are my own. I append, for comparison, metrical translations of three passages given in the text. The first and third are from a MS. of Prof. Herford's, and the second is from Mr. Archer's published translation of "Kongsemnerne." They will partly indicate how much has been sacrificed in adopting prose as the vehicle for rendering Ibsen's lyrics.

Finally, though I make no pretensions to a close and scholarly knowledge of the Dansk-Norsk language, I have reason to hope that few, if any, serious blunders will be found in my translations; for they have been very carefully and conscientiously revised by Fröken Kirstine Thaning of Copenhagen, to whom I am glad

---

[1] "Henrik Ibsen, 1828-1888." An English version of the German translation of this work has been executed by Miss Bell.

to have this opportunity of tendering my sincerest thanks.

P. H. W.

BRAND **ON DARKNESS.**

(See pp. 10, 11.)

Two thoughts in boyhood broke upon **me,**
　And spasms of laughter in me woke ;
And from our ancient school-dame won me
　Many a just and bitter stroke.
An Owl, I fancied, scared by Night ;
A Fish that had the water-fright ;
I sought to banish them ;—in vain,
They clung like leeches to my brain.
Whence rose that laughter in my mind ?
Ah, from the gulf, dimly divined,
Between the living world we see
And the world as it ought to be,
Between enduring what we must
And murmuring, It is unjust !

Ah, whole **or** sickly, great and small
Such owls, such fishes, are we all.
Born to be tenants of the deep,
Born to be exiles from the sun,
This, even this, does us appal ;

We dash against the beetling steep,
Our starry-vaulted home we shun,
And crying to heaven, bootless pray
For air, and the glad flames of day!

MARGRETE'S CRADLE SONG.

(See p. 16.)

Now roof and rafters blend with
   the starry vault on high ;
   now flieth little Hakon
   on dream-wings through the sky.

There mounts a mighty stairway
   from earth to God's own land ;
   there Hakon with the angels
   goes climbing, hand in hand.

God's angel-babes are watching
   thy cot, the still night through ;
   God bless thee, little Hakon,
   thy mother watcheth too.

EINAR AND AGNES.

(See pp. 32, 33.)

Einar. Agnes, my beautiful butterfly,
    Playfully shalt thou be caught ;
  I am weaving a net, and the meshes fine
    Are all of my music wrought.

Agnes. And am I a butterfly, dainty and small,
    Let me sip of the heatherbell blue ;
  And art thou a boy, let me be thy sport,
    But, oh! **not thy** captive too !

Einar. Agnes, my beautiful butterfly,
    I have woven my meshes so thin,
  And never availeth thy fluttering flight,
    Soon art **thou my** captive within.

Agnes. **And am I** a butterfly young and bright,
    Full joyously I can play,
  But **if** in thy net I'a captive lie,
    Oh, touch not my wings, I pray!

Einar. **Nay, I will lift** thee with tender hand
    And lock **thee up in my** breast,
  And there thou shalt **play** thy whole life long
    At the game thy heart loves **best** !

HENRIK IBSEN

LECTURE I.—THE POEMS.

IBSEN is a poet. His admirers claim for him that he
is a great deal more; but they base the claim upon
works which seem to those who are not his admirers
to establish a great deal less. I shall be content if in
this lecture I can give my hearers some of the materials
for a judgment on Ibsen's claim to the name of poet,
and, at the same time, point out sundry clues to the
meaning of his later writings which may be found in
his early poems.

But I must ask you to remember one thing—which
indeed there is little danger of your forgetting—namely,
that if Ibsen is a poet, I am none. The poems I shall
try to put before you will be robbed of the splendour
and depth of their colouring, and shorn of their rhyme,
they will have the pulsations of their metre tamed,
and, as far as form is concerned, will be but a mockery
of themselves. Yet, even so, I think they may be

A

trusted, and without further preface I will introduce
Ibsen's early

ARCHITECTURAL SCHEMES.

I remember as distinctly as if it had been this very
day, the night I saw my first printed poem in the paper.
There I sat in my den, 'midst the clouds I was puffing,
and smoked and dreamt in blessed self-complacency. "I
will build me a cloud castle. It shall gleam athwart the
North. Two gables shall there be there ; a great one and
a small. In the great one a deathless bard shall dwell ;
and the small one shall be a lady's bower." I thought
there was a glorious harmony in the conception ; but
afterwards some confusion crept in. As the master came
to his senses, the castle went clean crazy : the big gable
was too little, and the little one collapsed.

Many of Ibsen's poems are autobiographical, and it
is hardly hazardous to read into these lines (the suc-
cessive versions of which themselves contain a history)
the epitome of the author's poetic career. In those
days when the young apothecary was striving to make
good the defects of his early education, and was conscious of poetic powers struggling for utterance and
recognition, he probably conceived the task of the
poet much as other men did. Melodramatic and
romantic conceptions were in the air, and a "lady's
bower" was a quite necessary property for a rising
poet. But already strong elements of originality
manifested themselves in his ideas, and as he came to
his full powers he saw that the traditional motives and
materials of poetry were too narrow to give him scope,
and that "love poetry," as ordinarily understood, was

to occupy no place in his mature and serious work. "The big gable was too little—and the little one collapsed."

Brandes, the Danish critic, only repeats the testimony of these verses when he declares that sometime, in the course of the battle of his life, Ibsen had a Lyric Pegasus killed under him.

Let us look amongst the ruins of the little gable for a moment. Let us see if the hoof of Pegasus struck the soil anywhere, and left a Hippocrene to mark the spot.

GONE !

We followed the last guests to the wicket. The night wind swept away our last farewells. In ten-fold desolation lay the garden and house in which, but now, sweet tones had entranced me. It was only a festive meeting before the black night-fall; she was only one of the guests—and now gone ! she is gone !

Or let us turn to the verses sent—

WITH A WATERLILY.

See, my darling, what I've brought you. The flower with the white wings ! Borne on the quiet stream it floated dream-laden in the spring. Wouldst thou place it in its home, so lay it on thy breast, my darling ; for there a deep and silent wave will swell beneath its petals. Ah, child, beware of the mountain tarn stream ! There is danger, danger in dreaming there. The water-sprite pretends to sleep—and lilies play above. Child, thy bosom is the mountain tarn stream. There is danger, danger in dreaming there. Lilies play above—and the sprite pretends to sleep.

Or in a somewhat lighter vein we have—

A BIRD BALLAD.

We walked one lovely day in spring to and fro in the avenue; fascinating as a riddle was the forbidden spot. And the west wind was sighing, and the heaven was so blue! On the lime-tree sat a mother bird, singing to her brood. And I painted poet pictures with sportive colour-play; while two brown eyes were shining, laughing, and listening. And over above we could hear how they laughed and whispered at us. But we—we parted with a sweet farewell, never to meet again. And now when I wander all alone to and fro in the avenue, I can have neither rest nor peace for the little feathered folk. Dame sparrow sat there and listened as we walked in our innocence, and she made a poem about us and set it all to music. It's in the mouth of all the birds, for, under the foliage roof, every beaked songster twitters of that shining day in spring.

About contemporaneous with this poem was the composition of the "Gildet paa Solhaug," the brightest in tone and the happiest in its catastrophe of all Ibsen's plays. I will transcribe a song from it, less for its own sake than in order that the one bright picture in Ibsen's gallery may not be wholly unnoticed here.

I wandered on the hill-side, all heavy and alone, and from every bush and branch around twittered the little birds. So cunningly the little songsters sang: "Now listen while I tell how love doth spring! Though oak-like through long years it grows, nurtured by ponderings, sorrows, and songs, yet so quick does it shoot that a moment's space may fix its roots in the soil of the heart."

These specimens must suffice as samples of Ibsen's love poetry, but there is one splendid example of melodrama that has borne him over all the Scandinavian countries as a popular poet, something as Browning's "Pied Piper," and "How they brought the good news from Ghent to Aix," took hold of the popular fancy when his more characteristic work was practically unread. We do not readily think of Ibsen in connection with "Penny Readings," but yet "Terje Vigen," the hero of the longest of his minor poems, is ideally framed to figure at those humble entertainments.

Terje Vigen is a Norwegian sailor, who after a more or less wild and wandering life marries, and finds the constraints of a settled life converted into the supremest happiness when a little daughter laughs up at him from her cradle. But the wars of the early part of this century reduce his Norwegian village to direst distress. The British fleet cuts off all supplies from without, and the harvest fails at home. Terje takes the desperate resolve to row over to Denmark in an open boat to get food for his wife and child. As he returns, and is close at home, he is sighted by an English man-of-war and pursued by a boat with fifteen men. He rows till the blood bursts from his finger nails to clear a rock two feet below the water on which the heavier boat of his pursuers may strike; but just as he is clearing it the English come up, and the young officer raises an oar and strikes a hole in Terje's boat. His three precious casks of barley are lost and he is taken prisoner, to the immense delight of the young Englishman, who laughs at his outlandish attempts to plead for his liberty and the life of his dear ones, and carries him off in triumph to the man-of-war.

It is years before the peace puts an end to Terje's captivity, and when he returns home it is to hear that " when her husband deserted her," the woman died, and so did her child ; and they had a pauper burial.

Thenceforth Terje, grey-headed with the anguish he has suffered, and with his neck bent as in shame, is the most daring and skilful of pilots ; and on a certain stormy night he is summoned to the aid of a distressed English yacht. He is just bringing her off when he sees "my lord" with " my lady " and their beautiful child. Then he lets the yacht go, declares that she will not obey the helm, thrusts the three with himself into a boat, rows them into quieter waters, then stands erect, seizes an oar, strikes a hole in the bottom of the boat, and they are all standing in two feet of water far from the shore.

Then my lord cried out, " The rock gives way ! It can be no rock at all." But the pilot smiled. " Nay, be sure of that ! A sunken boat and three barley casks are the rock that bears us now." Then swept the memory of a half-forgotten deed like a lightning flash o'er the Englishman's face, as he knew the sailor that once knelt weeping on the deck of his corvette. Then Terje Vigen shouted aloud : " You held my all in your hand that day, and for glory you squandered it all. One moment more and revenge will have come."

It was then that the haughty Englishman bent his

knee to the Norsk pilot. But Terje stood straight, as in days of youth, as he steadied himself with the oar; through his eyes flamed out his untamed force, and his hair streamed out on the wind:—

"You sailed at your ease, in your great corvette, and I rowed my little boat; I was toiling for dear ones, wearied to death, and you took their bread, and you thought so lightly of mocking my bitter tears. Your rich lady there is as bright as spring, and her hand is as soft as silk; and my wife's hand it was coarse and hard, but, she was my own, my wife. Your child has golden hair and blue eyes like a little guest of the Lord; and my daughter was nothing to look upon, for she—God help her—was sallow and lean as most poor folk's little ones are. But they were the sum of my earthly wealth, they were all that I called my own. They seemed such a mighty treasure to me, and with you so little they weighed. And now has the hour of recompense struck, for you shall go through such an hour as well may balance the whole long years that bowed my neck and that bleached my hair, and that ran my bliss a-ground."

Then he seized the child and he swung him free, and his left arm the lady clasped.

"Stand back, my lord! One step in advance will cost you your child and wife!"

And the Briton was ready to spring to the fight, but his arm fell palsied and weak; his breath came burning, his eye drooped down, and his hair—as the dawning showed next day—turned grey in that single night. But on Terje's brow there was calmness and peace, and his breast was free and still, and in reverence laid he the baby down, and its hands he gently kissed. And he breathed as if loosed from a prison's vault, and his voice came steady and calm—

"Now is Terje Vigen himself again. Till now my

blood flowed like a river stone-rent ; for I *must*, I *must* be avenged ! . . . But now it is over ; we two are quits. Your debtor has played you fair. I gave what I could ; you took all I had,—and now if you think you've been wronged by me, then make your complaint to the Lord above, for He made me the way I am."

In the end, of course, Terje brings them all safe to shore, and when thanked as their preserver, points to the child. It was she that saved them.

But it is time we left the common ground on which Ibsen comes into comparison with so many of his brethren ; for we shall find in his poems many a weird foreshadowing of the motives of his later work.

Quite an early poem gives a powerful presentment of that almost passionate belief that light may be found in and through darkness, alternating with apparent acquiescence in the darkness itself, which fascinates and repels the readers of the social dramas.

THE MINER.

Mine-wall! break with crash and clang before my heavy hammer-strokes. Downward must I break my way till I hear the ore-stones ring. Deep in the mountain's waste of night rich treasure beckons me, diamond and precious stone, amidst the gold's red veins. And in the deep is peace, peace and desolation from eternity ; break me the way, my heavy hammer, to the hidden mystery's heart.[1] Erst I sat, a merry boy, under the heaven's host of stars, or trod the flowery way of spring,

---

[1] Lit. "the heart-chamber of the Hidden." Compare Job xxviii. with the whole poem.

with child-peace for my own. But I forgot the glory of day, as I turned to the midnight darkness, forgot the soughing and song of the hillside in the temple arcade of my mine. When first I came down hither, in innocence of heart I deemed that the spirit of the depth would read me the endless riddle of life. As yet no spirit has unravelled for me what seemed to me so strange ; as yet no ray has risen, gleaming upward from the ground. Have I failed then ? Will my chosen way never lead me through to the clear ? Yet the light blinds my eyes when I seek it above. Nay, I must down into the depth ; there is peace from eternity. Break me the way, my heavy hammer, to the hidden mystery's heart. Hammer stroke on hammer stroke, on till life's last day. No beam of morning shines. No sun of hope arises.

What are we to say to this strange affinity with darkness ? The shy and sensitive poet, neglected or made light of by the literary coteries and the critics of his day, barely able to secure his daily bread, feeling as though the light were not for him, learns to love the darkness and strives to find its peace, its light, its hope if it may be—its peace in any case. Can he here find the scope that seems to be denied him in the world of light ?

AFRAID OF THE LIGHT.

In my schoolboy days I had pluck enough,—at least till the sun went down behind the mountain ridge. But when the shadows of night stretched over hill and marsh, then ugly hobgoblins scared me from sagas and fairy

tales.   And no sooner did I close my eyes than I dreamt,
and dreamt, and dreamt, and all my pluck had left me
and had gone to God knows where.   But now everything
has changed with me.   Now my courage sets off on its
wanderings when the morning sunshine comes.   Now
'tis the troubles of the day and the bustle of life that drip
all the cold horrors into my breast.   I hide myself under
a flap of the scarecrow veil of the dark, and there all my
courage arms itself as eagle-bold as ever.   Then I defy
flame and fire, I sail like a falcon in the cloud, I forget
all my care and woe till the next morning dawn.   But
when the protection of night fails me I am helpless and
lost again.   Yea, if I shall e'er do a heroic deed it must
needs be a deed of the dark.

Readers of " Brand " will remember how this strange
motive reappears there.   Through all the passion for
light and air that beats through the poem there runs a
suspicion—sometimes faint and forgotten, sometimes
resented and fought against, sometimes felt as a crush-
ing and deadening weight, sometimes accepted as a
faith in which alone is strength and rest—that man
was made for the peace and depth of darkness, not
for the glare of light, and that the longing for happiness is but the monstrous disease of a creature sick to
leave its own natural element.

Two ideas [says Brand], used to drop into my mind
as a boy, and shake my frame with fits of laughter, and
get me a tanned hide when the old school-dame was out
of temper.   I used to fancy myself an owl afraid of the
dark, and a fish with a horror of water.   I laughed aloud
at the idea ; and strove to smuggle it out of my mind, but

it stuck there with tooth and claw. What was it caused these bursts of laughter? It was a confused sense of the incongruity between the thing as it is and the thing as it ought to be, between the fact of our having to bear and our finding the burden unbearable. Almost every man that walks, sick or sound, is such an owl, is such a fish. Created for abysmal deeds, he should have lived with life's dark depths—and that is just what scares him. He spralls in eager longing on the edge of the tide. He shuns his own star chamber. And shrieks out for "air and the blazing day !"

In the period of seething and ferment to which most of the " poems " belong, we find other indications that the disappointed, disillusionised, almost starving poet strove in many moods to find the highest life in an existence cut off from the sympathy, the appreciation, the expansion, the full personal utterance, that seemed to be denied him.

In a poem that in the original almost freezes the blood, we have a kind of prelude to Peer Gynt. Ibsen makes the characteristic attempt to extract the highest life out of a cynicism, driven to an extreme at which the most hardened must shudder, and out of the absolute death of all that most call life. Here, as often elsewhere, we are left in doubt whether the concluding lines are intended as a real solution, or only as the last and bitterest satire. The hero of " On the Viddes,"[1] like Peer Gynt after him, strives at first to

---

[1] A " Vidde " is a high stretch of mountain land, the home of the rein-deer and bear.

make good his trespasses by cheap regrets and re-
solutions that cost nothing.   He lies high up on the
hill-side the night after he has parted with his be-
trothed ;

And thoughts they came and thoughts they went like
folk on church-way path ; gathered in knots and gazed
around, set up the judgment-seat and uttered doom, and
stalked in silence by.   Oh were I near thee in this
hour, thou flower I broke yestreen, I would lay me down
like a faithful hound before thy garment's hem.   Right
into thine eyes I would I float, and there would I cleanse
my soul ; and the trold that bewitched my soul last night
as I stood by thy father's gate I would smite to death in
scorn !

Then glowing with the sense of victory he leaps up
and first offers a winged prayer to God that on all his
dear bride's days sunshine may ever lie ; but then as
the sense of strength mounts in him he prays rather
that her path may be hard, the river dammed when
she would cross, the rock slippery, the pathway steep,
that he may bear her on his arm across the torrent and
clasp her close to his breast, where God himself shall
not hurt her unchallenged or unresisted !

Then on the Vidde he meets his own mysterious
second self in the form of a stranger who lays a spell
upon him that he would oft have broken if he could,
that he does not now even wish to break.   This man,
with the unspoken thoughts, gleaming like the northern
dawn around his brow, with tears in his laughter, and
lips that move when he is silent, in utterance as
mysterious as the song of the wind through the trees,

terrifies and fascinates him with his cold eye as un-
fathomable as the darkling tarn fed and clasped by the
bosom of the great snow-fields. Heavy thought-
birds sweep low over the face of this man's mind, or
it is torn by wild storms whereat you lower sail and
crouch in terror for your very life. Ever seeming to
stand for a wider, freer, and nobler life, and representing himself as an uplifting force, he gradually weans
our hero from all his home thoughts and longings,
till at last he learns to be ashamed of every old affection and to trample upon his own humanity as mere
sentimentalism. At last the freezing cynicism of
his other self has found such a lodgment that it can
assert itself even under the shadow of a sorrow or a
passion that rends his very soul. He is gazing down
at his mother's cottage, and a sneer from the stranger
has determined him never again to yield to such
weakness, when he sees a glow round roof and rail:
first it is like a cloudy dawn, then the red flame bursts
through.

It shone and it flamed and it crashed into ruins, and
I shrieked my agony into the night; but the stranger had
comfort: "Why so disturbed? I suppose it's only the old
house burning, with the Christmas ale and the cat!" He
talked with such skill in all my woe that it well-nigh made
me shudder; and he pointed out the striking effect of the
fiery glow as it streamed out into moonbeam's light, with
two-fold illumination. He looked at it through his
hollowed hand to secure the right perspective; while a
song swept over the rock and snow, and I knew full well
that my mother's soul into angel hands was being given;
" In stillness thou toiledst, in stillness didst bear, and went

thy still way through the turmoil; so we bear thee all
gently away from the earth, high o'er the Vidde to light
and to peace, to the joy of the Christmas in heaven!"
The hunter was gone, the moon hidden in cloud, and
my blood was on fire and freezing. O'er the Vidde I
bore my anguish-load.—But it can't be denied that it
was effective, that two-fold illumination!

It only remains for him to feel the last pang as a
bridal procession goes out from another cottage, and
he recognises in the bride her who was to have been his.

Joy go with thee, my sweetest! Now I have played
my last stake and gained a loftier outlook upon things.
Now I am steeled, and shall follow the summons that
bids me stride out o'er the mountains! My life in the
valleys has been lived out. Up here on the Vidde are
freedom and God! All the rest are but fumbling down
there.

A terrible story of bitterness and disappointment
may be read in such lines as these. But what suppressed passion and intensity of life through it all, and
what Titanic strength! If anyone finds in such
cynicism—blood-curdling as I have called it—mere
frivolity or "Leichtzinnigkeit," he mistakes a deadly
determination to endure for a want of sensibility.
Here, if ever, the words of a German admirer are
applicable, "Ibsen ist so furchtbar ernst."

In truth, Ibsen was in the valley of the shadow of
death at the period when his chief poems were
written. He was fighting for his very life, both
literally and metaphorically. He himself associates
verse-writing and suffering together in a grimly

humorous poem, which may serve to relieve us after
" Paa Vidderne."

THE POWER OF MEMORY.

Listen here! Do you know how a trainer teaches
his bear a lesson he never forgets? He ties the beast up
in a brewer's vat and they light a fire right under it.
Meanwhile the trainer plays, " Oh, happy, happy life ! "
on the barrel organ, for the bear to hear. The hairy
monster is almost beside himself with pain. He can't
stand still, so he has to dance. And ever after, as soon as
he hears that tune, he's possessed by a dancing devil. I
myself once sat in a copper with a full accompaniment,
and a very respectable temperature. And on that occasion
I burnt myself more than skin-deep, and I don't suppose
I shall ever forget it. And whenever an echo of that
time comes over me I feel as if I were chained in a red-
hot copper. I know it like a thrust under the roots of the
nails—and I can't choose but hop on my metrical feet.

But through all this period Ibsen still had a refuge
in an ideal world. He had begun his practical
dramatic career with a play founded on the darkest
period of Norwegian history. Then he had ascended
to the fourteenth century, the ballad period. Then
he had idealised the Viking period in a play of extreme beauty, founded on the story of the Volsung
saga, and finally had dramatised the great historical
motives of the period following upon Harold Fair-
hair's unification of Norway. Would that Englishmen could have learnt to know Ibsen first by " The

Vikings of Helgeland" and "The Pretenders"! These noble dramas are now accessible in translations, and I will, therefore, refrain from any attempt to indicate their general character and significance. But the man who, in the midst of such feelings and experiences as we have seen reflected in the "poems," could conceive not only a Hjördis and a Skule, but a Dagny, a Sigurd, a Margrete, and a Ingebjörg, had surely not lost all sense of quiet beauty and tenderness, even as judged by us "fumblers down here below"!

Let us listen for one moment to Margrete's "Cradle Song," before we plunge again into the deep waters.

Now roof and rafter open out to the blue star-vault above. With dream-wings on his shoulders, flies little Haakon up. Upon the earth a ladder that reaches heaven is set and little Haakon rises with angels to the top. God's angels small are watching over the baby's peace; God bless thee, little Haakon, thy mother shares their watch.

In King Skule, critics have agreed in recognising many traits of Ibsen's own character and experiences. Perhaps in his last speech we may find an indication of the crisis through which the poet was now passing. All his surroundings seemed to be hostile and cramping. He panted for life and scope. He sought refuge in the great memories of the past, though with an eye more and more fixed on the present. Did that present really offer him a life and scope to which he was somehow blind? The dying Skule sees at last that in the love of his wife and daughter he had, and knew it not, the treasure for which he ranged the world in sin and devastation. Has each man his true mission close at hand, if he could but see with his eyes? Had Ibsen himself a poetic call for the present rather than the past? Had he sources of strength which could well enable him to defy the neglect and opposition that were embittering his life? There was one already standing at his side, to whom after many years he wrote his words of

THANKS.

The griefs that made rugged my way were her sorrow, the spirit-beings that bore me forward were her joy. Her home is out here on the ocean of freedom, where the poet's bark may lie mirrored. The rank of shifting forms that march with waving banners through my verse are her kin. Her goal is to kindle my sight into glow, while none can know who gave me the help. And just because she looks not even for thanks must I sing her, and print her this thankful song.

But if Ibsen was to be the poet of his own time, it must be in his own way. And what that way should be is again indicated in a remarkable passage in "The Pretenders."

King Skule's heart is gnawed by doubts as to his right and as to his rival's right. Were he sure of either, he thinks, he could be at peace. He doubts his own power and worthiness for kingship, but he doubts it doubtingly. He is questioning the skald

B

Jatgeir, whose answers strike deeper than he himself
knows, and answer more than the questions that
provoke them.

    K. Skule.   Tell me, Jatgeir, how came you to be a
bard?   Who taught you the art?

    Jatgeir.   The art cannot be taught, sire.

    K. Skule.   It cannot be taught?   Then how came
it?

    Jatgeir.   One gave me the gift of sorrow, and so I
became a bard.

    K. Skule.   Then is the gift of sorrow what a bard
needs?

    Jatgeir.   It was what I needed.   Another may need
faith, or joy, or doubt.

    K. Skule.   Doubt! can it be that?

    Jatgeir.   Yes! but then the doubter must be strong
and crisp.

    K. Skule.   And what do you mean by a limp doubter?

    Jatgeir.   One who doubts his own doubt.

    K. Skule (slowly).   That, methinks, were death.

    Jatgeir.   Worse! worse!   It were life in death![1]

Place side by side with this scene the "Rhymed
Epistle," printed near the end of Ibsen's collected
poems. A friend has asked him what is the matter
with the present age which, with all its resources and
all its strength, seems to be haunted by a vague appre-
hension, and to have its vigour sapped by some secret
spirit of dulness and weariness. Ibsen answers,
characteristically enough, that he prefers asking ques-

---

[1] Literally "twilight."

tions, and that it is not his mission to answer them. For once, however, he will try to say how the thing looks to him. Sailors have a superstition against making a voyage with a corpse on board. If a suspicion gets about that there is a dead body somewhere in the cargo, all becomes spiritless and slack, and there is no spring or confidence in the crew. Ibsen compares life to a good ship on her voyage. He is one of the passengers himself.

I was sitting here alone upon the deck one sultry night, with the stars and silence for company. The breeze was as soft and gentle as may be, for the wings of the evening wind were clipped. All the passengers had gone to their berths, and the lamp burned sleepily down below. A stifling hot air flowed up from the cabin, and held its weary victims in a half slumber. Their sleep was restless and unpeaceful, as I could see through the half-opened swing glass of the skylight. Here lay a statesman, twisting his mouth as if for a smile, but it ended in a yawn. There a learned professor tossed from side to side, quarrelling, it seemed, with his own learning. A theologian dragged the bed-clothes over his head ; and another man was burrowing into his pillow. High and low there lay artists, authors, like folk in a dream, fearing and expectant. But over all this half sleeping life below brooded a lurid, steaming, stifling heat. I averted my eye from all the weary turmoil. I gazed out into the fresh night. I looked eastward where the faint dawn was already beginning to veil the brightness of the stars. Then a sound struck my ear from there below ; it struck me as I sat leaning against the mast. Someone cried out, half-way, it seemed, between an uneasy sleep and a nightmare, " I believe we're sailing with a corpse in the cargo."

There we have it! What is the corpse? What is the dead matter we are carrying with us? Is it the inheritance from our ancestors? Is it our commercial system? Is it our marriage laws? Is it our confirmed habit of lying? Is it the foolish and narrow way in which we speak the truth when we give it a turn? Is it our untamed elemental passions not yet humanized? Is it our traditional and conventional pretences? Is it our religion?

If any man is afraid of these questions let him give Ibsen a wide berth. If any man dares to ask them without reserve, let him welcome the terrible "poet of doubt," and listen to his questionings without demanding that he shall answer as well as ask them.

Ibsen is the poet of doubt. What is his mission, and what must be his qualifications? He must be a whole-hearted doubter. He must not feel responsible for giving answers, or he will tone down his questioning to the compass of his answering powers. But above all he must be neither a cynic nor a sentimentalist, else how can he put true questions? Under and through them all we must feel unfailing discernment of beauty, and loyalty to truth, undulled responsiveness of soul to generosity and nobility, a determination not to accept as answers what are no answers at all, and a tender reverence for every thought or impulse that bears in itself such *life*, that the poet doubter needs not question it.

Ibsen is the poet of doubt; and his doubting is so strong and true that, when we have dealt with the questions he asks us, we shall have dealt with life.

But at the period we have already reached—the period of the publication of "The Pretenders" in 1863—Ibsen was still able to live an ideal life in the great traditions of Norway, and had not yet been forced to accept his mission as the poet of doubt. It was in Norwegian history and legend that he found the subjects of almost all his dramas, and it was here that he found again the Norway, brave and strong, which he could hardly recognise amid the petty interests, and the sordid jealousies, and disputes of his immediate surroundings. In his love of the glorious memories of the past he was at one with those from whom he was divided in all else.

When the Dano-German War was impending, the memories of Norway's heroic age revived in every breast. The King of Norway and Sweden had pledged himself to the King of Denmark, wild enthusiasm reigned among the youthful Norwegians, and the cause of Scandinavia seemed to be one.

But when the test came prudence prevailed over enthusiasm. The King, to his bitter grief it is said, was forced to draw back from his word. Sweden and Norway took no part in the struggle. No stream of volunteers flowed southward. It was looked upon as a mere piece of useless Quixotism to throw into the scale a weight that could not turn it. The Norwegians were a poor and feeble nation. What could they do against the overwhelming power of the foe?

So Denmark was left to fight and fall alone.

Ibsen sounded the alarm-bell over Norway in a

poem which the older generation of Danes cannot read dry-eyed to this day.

Now round the fort of Tyra gathers—maybe for the last time—a folk under strain and grief, with flag hung half-mast high. Deserted, deserted in the day of peril, deserted in the hour of strife! Was this the meaning of the clasp of hands so rich in promise for the Northern cause at Axelstad and Sound?

The words that flowed as from the heart were but a gush of phrases, and now the well is dry. The tree that blossomed into vows in the sunshine of a festal day stands stripped by the storm wind, like a cross to mark the grave of Norway's youth, the first night that calls for work!

They were but dressed-up lies, a poisoned Judas kiss, that Norway's sons shouted but now in exultation towards the beach of Sound. What passed 'twixt King and King at the last royal journey? It was only King Gustave once again playing at the game of Charles the Twelfth's sword in Stockholm Castle.

"A grieving folk on the path of death, deserted by every friend—" So ends the book of Denmark's history. Who is it wrote the close? What coward suffered such an end, and let Tyra's fort turn German, while Denmark's rent flag wrapped its red folds round the last Danish corpse?

But thou, my Norsk brother, in thy safety, standing in a land of peace, thanks to thy fair words of promise forgotten in the hour of danger, flee from the gathering places of thy sires, haste o'er the ocean's arch, tread from harbour to harbour the path of forgetfulness, take on thee a stranger's name, and hide from thy very self!

The breath of every storm that sweeps to Norway

from the shores of Denmark's sea, strikes thee with horror as it sighs, " My brother, where art thou ? I strove a strife of life and death for the northern lands, and my home became a grave ; I gazed over belt and fiord all in vain to see thy war-ships' trace. My brother, where art thou ?"

It was a dream. Wake strong and brave—a people roused from slumbering to deeds ! A brother's need ! All hands on deck ! Swift counsel need we now ! Yet may it stand in history: " Danes, Danes, hold Tyra's fort." Yet may the tattered flag of Denmark wave its red folds rich over the future of the North !

But as we all know it was the last stanza, not the others, that was the dream ; and the Danes fought and fell alone. Ibsen could no longer take refuge in Norway's past, for the measure of its former glory had become to him the measure of its present shame ; and every thought of the heroic past was turned to bitterness.

At this very time Ibsen lost the means by which he earned his scanty rations, for the theatre with which he was connected failed, owing to want of sufficient interest in the national Norwegian drama.

There is a custom in Norway of making parliamentary grants to distinguished or promising authors, to enable them to travel. Ibsen applied for a grant and obtained it, but it was given him half as a charity.

Sick at heart he turned southwards and felt that he could never return. Home life was poisoned for him. In burning shame and indignation at what he considered his country's disgrace, **stung by** personal insults, **and** embittered by **disappointment, he** stood, as he himself expresses it, "on the edge of **his grave** as a poet." **But it** was **out of the very** heart of all this bitterness that **he** produced **the** two great poems that **took Norway** and all Scandinavia by storm, and established his fame beyond the reach **of** cavil.

These poems **were** "Brand" **and** "**Peer** Gynt," **and in** them, together with "The Youthful League," **which followed,** Ibsen **poured out** the vials **of his wrath.**

The frame of mind in which he left **his home and composed** his great **lyric** dramas, together **with** the gradual softening **of his** feelings towards **his** fatherland, and the **yearning of his heart** towards the North, **may be** traced **in** the group **of** poems with which **I** shall conclude this lecture.

First—in immediate connection with the poem just transcribed—comes :

WELL GROUNDED FAITH.

I swung the alarm bell **over the** land **in** my rhymes— **but** no one was the least alarmed. My **part** was played ; I embarked on **a** steamer and left **the "dear North"** behind me. We lay to in **a** fog in Kattegat and **no** one slept the first night. A council **of** war was **held in** the cabin, and **the** passengers talked **of the** fall of Dybböl. **They** discussed everything, and **told** sundry tales **of the wild** doings of the young volunteers. **One** had lost a nephew eighteen years old, another had lost his shop assistant. It really became quite touching, and **I** was **more** or less affected myself. On the sofa right under the lamp-shade sat a lady of advanced age, dauntless and unshaken. Most of the company addressed their words to her and vied with each other in offering her comfort. And the ladies, with sigh and moan, expressed their anxiety for her only son. I can see her still, so confidently nodding and smiling as she said, " I've no fear for him!" How beautiful she looked with her silvered hair and the rooted faith in her heart. A warm glow coursed through blood and marrow, and my drooping courage was steeled. " Thy people is not dead, e'en though it slumber; it lives in the miracle of woman's faith ! " But afterwards I found she was better skilled in the ways of the world than the " way of life." And so she became a riddle to me. Where did it spring from, this grace of confidence ? The explanation was as plain as the nose on your face. Her son was a warrior in the *Norwegian* army !

In marked contrast of tone, is the more celebrated poem entitled :—

THE EIDER-DUCK.

In Norway the eider-duck dwells, and his home is the lead-grey fiord. He plucks the soft down from his breast and builds his nest warm and snug. But the fiord fisherman has a heart of steel, and he plunders the nest to the very last mote. If the fisherman is cruel, the bird's love is warm ; he strips his own breast once more. And if plundered again, he yet once more lines his nest in a well-hidden nook. But if his third treasure, his last, be robbed, then he spreads his wings on a spring night ; then he cleaves the clouds with his bleeding breast, southward, southward, to lands of the sun !

Ibsen felt that he had definitively broken with his own land as a home, but he belonged to it still.

BURNT SHIPS.

Southward he turned his vessel's prow, and sought the
sportive track of brighter gods. The snow land's mountains sank in the sea, his longings were rocked into stillness by the sun-lit strands. He burned his ships ; and
the smoke-cloud drifted blue towards the north like a
bridge-way.—To the huts of the snow land, from the groves
of the south, all alone rides a horseman each night as
night comes.

Yet more explicit is the opening of the poem written
in 1872 on the occasion of the millenary feast of
Norway's unification.

My folk, that gave me in deep shoals the wholesome,
bitter, strengthening drink, wherefrom, standing on the
brink of my grave as a poet, I received strength for the
fight amidst the broken lights of daily life,—my folk
that reached me the exile's staff, the burden of sorrow
and the swift shoes of care, the sad and solemn equipment
for my journey,—home from the world I send thee back
a greeting—send it with thanks for all thy gifts, with
thanks for the cleansing-tide of every anguish. For each
plant that has thriven in the garden of my calling
stands rooted deep in those same times. If here it shoot
in fulness wealth and joy, it owes it to the grey blasts
blowing in the North. What sunshine loosened mists
made firm! Have thanks, my land—thy gift to me was
best. Yea! there where the mists roll over the rock-peaks,
where the blasts smite bleak upon the Vidde, where
echoing silence reigns over hut and hill, where between
farm and farm stretches the waste, thither I gaze like the
pilot from the deck-bridge. At night and in my poems I
belong to home.

LECTURE II.—" BRAND."

WHEN Ibsen turned his back upon "the dear North,' and tried to forget the life that lay behind him, he bathed his soul for a time in the warmth and beauty of Italy.

His thoughts and studies turned to the ancient world, and he planned and partly executed the work that afterwards grew into the two plays, of which Julian the Apostate is the hero.

But the spell of the North was still upon him. It forced his mind back to the bleak and chill home of his childhood with all its freezing memories. The unfinished work was set aside, and before it was taken up again and completed, "Brand," " Peer Gynt," and "The Youthful League" had flowed in rapid succession from Ibsen's pen.

In " Brand" the poet turns fiercely upon his native land, but amid all his passion and contempt learns and tells the truth that there is no redeeming power save in love.

Brand is a young Norwegian clergyman, to whom the heroic age has vanished, and who regards his contemporaries as a paltry, timorous, and sordid race, who plead their own self-inflicted feebleness as the excuse for shrinking from every sacrifice, who believe they have been stamped as farthings in the mint of God, and are content to have it so, and who are yet not content to give up all pride in the past, and all aspirations for the future, and frankly own themselves the slaves of earth. He finds them striving to be a little of everything, to have a little faith and earnestness for use on Sundays, a little patriotism for national anniversaries, a little hilarity and good-fellowship for festive occasions after work, a little recklessness and abandon in making promises, a little caution and sobriety in fulfilling them, a little attachment to the good old times and their customs and memories, a little perception of the changed spirit of their own day. Their life is all broken up into fragments, and each fragment hampers, contradicts, deadens all the rest so that they can never live a full *life*.

Their religion is in perfect keeping with all this. One might, perhaps, think that their very materialism had, at least, given unity to their lives—but no, it is haunted and broken by memories of a spiritual religion that make a discord with it. Men still repeat the Lord's Prayer, but there is not a line of it that is winged with will and has in it such deep and anxious insistence of demand as will launch it heavenwards with the full ring of prayer, save the fourth petition : "Give us this day our daily bread." This has become the people's war-cry and the password of the world. Wrenched from its context and stamped upon every heart this prayer remains—the storm-tossed spar that tells of the wreck of faith ! Yet this very survival is the testimony that men are not contentedly and whole-heartedly material. They snip and trim the kingdom of God till it can all get inside the Church walls, but they must have "a little" of it. They have none of the fresh manhood of faith that can bridge over the chasm between spirit and flesh, but they still haggle for "a little" of the spiritual consolations now dealt out in retail by the ecclesiastical hucksters. "A little" idealism and spiritual exaltation is quite essential as an element in their existence.

Into such a society Brand leaps with his awful and heroic motto, "all or nothing," and in the name of the jealous deity who "will have no other gods by his side," seeks to build up human nature into unity, to remake, out of these stumps of soul and torsos of spirit, out of these scattered heads and hands, such a whole that God may be able to recognise once more his noblest work in man.

For the current religion Brand has neither sympathy nor even pity—nothing but scorn. The God men worship is a superannuated and feeble dotard, that did miracles long ago, and was once a jealous God, but is now quite easy-going, and content with his fragment of the human heart, willing enough to accept the service of one day out of seven, and altogether past working miracles. The very doctrine of Christian redemption has made men look upon themselves as no longer called upon for any sacrifice as long as they formally assert their claim to a share in the great sacrifice made for them long ago.

Against this miserable, sordid, and decrepid religion Brand declares war to the death. · Better become frankly material and godless, better give oneself up to the world and become an acknowledged muck-raker on the one hand, or Bacchanal on the other, than cheat oneself with such a sham. It must be "everything or nothing," and if there be a God to serve, then his service must be "everything." And such a God

there is.   If we must picture him under human form,
then he is no benevolent and weak old man; he is
young and strong as Hercules, his love is the love
that could listen to the prayer of anguish in Gethse-
mane and yet *not* take away the cup.   He demands
the whole life and will accept no less.   He who offers
God one-seventh, or one-half, or nine-tenths of his
life flings it into the abyss—it must be *all* or *nothing*.
Brand's God can still work miracles, and the life that
is given wholly to him may still be divinely harmonious as of old.

When we first see Brand he is fired with the
thought of preaching this living God to all the world,
and, as he contemptuously puts it, burying the dead
God that men still profess to worship.

With the so-called " practical " spirit of the age he
has little sympathy, still less with its tolerant and
humane culture.   Its "practical" spirit means putting
material things before spiritual, with the poor hope
of achieving a true humanity by means of in-
creased material appliances.   It thinks a new road
and a new bridge of more pressing consequence than
a bridge between faith and life, fails to see that until
we are men we heap up wealth in vain, and if we are
men we do not need it.   And the humane and tolerant spirit of the age is only a fine name for indifference to truth, for weak shrinking from giving or
bearing pain, for dissipation of energy,—for the devil's
breath of compromise and cowardice.

To this man, with his motto "all or nothing,"
there is no common measure between material and

spiritual things. You may stay your steps on God's errands because you *can* not go farther, but never because you *dare* not, or because you *will* not. If his way leads him over the crevasse-crossed glacier, and the mists fall upon him as the ice rings thin and hollow beneath his feet, and the roar of the hidden waters threatens him with instant death, he has no thought of pausing or turning back. It is enough for him that he *can* go farther, and while his peasant guide leaves him in mortal terror, though his dying daughter lies on the other side of the snow-field and can not be at peace without seeing him, the intrepid priest, with no reason to cross to-day rather than to-morrow, save that each day is a day to be devoted to his mission, pursues his way.

No physical suffering moves him. He passes untouched through the starving town, where the blue-grey ring round every hollow eye shows that death is holding his assize, and is only moved to a deeper scorn when he sees that the scourge brings out the brute rather than the angel in the sufferers. But a tale of the mental anguish of a father who has slain his child that he might not see it starve, and now himself lies dying, stirs him to deepest compassion, and in a storm through which even the wife of the dying man dare not venture with him, he crosses the fiord in an open boat to stand by the bed of the murderer and suicide as the messenger of God.

Then the call comes to him to relinquish all his thoughts of a crusading march through his land, and an attack in the face of all the world upon the idols it

serves, and to bury himself in a sunless town on a remote fiord, where the memory of his lonely childhood
broods like night over his soul, where his miserly
mother, who bartered away her soul for wealth in her
early days, and hopes to save it in her old age by
dedicating her son to the Church, oppresses him with
her unreclaimed sordidness, and where every influence
seems most hostile to his life-work.

And yet in truth the sacrifice is no sacrifice at
all. For Agnes has already convinced him that
his crusade must be fought out at home and not
abroad.

And who is Agnes? We see her first, with her
lover, Einar, the painter and poet, in the sunshine
and beauty of the morning on the hill-side.

Einar. Agnes, my beautiful butterfly, thee will I
capture in sport! I am weaving a net with meshes so
fine, and the meshes so fine are my songs.

Agnes [*dancing back before him and darting out of
his reach*]. If I'm a butterfly little and fine, then let me
still sip from the ling-bloom; and if you are a boy that
delights in his game, then chase me, but catch me not
ever.

Einar. Agnes, my beautiful butterfly, now have I
woven the meshes; sure your fluttering flight will avail
you naught—soon you sit in the net fairly captured.

Agnes. If I'm a butterfly young and bright, rejoicing
I swing in the sport; but should I be caught 'neath your
woven net, then brush not against my wings.

Einar. Nay! With such care on my hand will I
lift thee, and lock thee right into my heart; and there

shalt thou play thy whole life long the gladest of games thou e'er knewest.

But when Agnes hears Brand speak of the feebleness and poverty of the age and of the stern gospel it needs, she wakes from her butterfly existence as from a dream. It is in vain that Einar strives to pick up the thread of sport where they dropped it. Agnes answers him without hearing, and in her turn asks, without looking at him, in a hushed whisper as if in church : "But tell me, did you see—how he *grew* while he was speaking?" Then when Brand is ready to cross the storm-torn fiord and none dares to go with him, Agnes bids Einar join him, and when he shrinks back in terror the whole world-ocean stretches between him and her. She herself leaps into the boat and braves the storm with Brand.

When he leaves the death-bed to which he had come to stand between the dying sinner and his fighting soul he sees Agnes sitting in the clear sunshine, rapt as if in a vision.

See how there she sits and listens, as to songs that fill the welkin. In the boat she sat and listened, as it cleft the troubled waters ; as she grasped the thwart she listened, listened as she shook the storm-spray from her clear, unclouded forehead. 'Twas as though the sense had changed its seat, and with her eyes she listened.

What is her vision, as she sits there listening with her eyes? She sees the crude forces of an unborn world, with its torrents, its clouds, its lightning glow, its wild

winds, its desert stretches, its unmeasured possibilities,
waiting to be created—and created by her! For in
her own breast she recognises its counterpart in the
swelling of untamed forces like mountain torrents, in
the rising light of the new day, in the widening of the
reach of life, in the new quickening and movement of
thought and deed, as though their hour of birth had
come, in the sadness and the joy that are as one, in
the divine voice that rings in her ears, "Now shalt thou
create, now be created! Now art thou redeemed or
lost! Do thy work—thy work of dear account."

When Einar comes and claims her once again she
stands between him and Brand. Brand warns her
that he is uncompromising in his demands, requiring
"all or nothing," that if she fails half way, then all her
life will have been flung into the sea, that she must
look for no concession in time of need, no yielding to
any weakness, that if her life-strength falls short she
must face death itself. Einar cries to her that she is
choosing between storm and calm, between peace and
sorrow, between night and morning, between life and
death. And she answers, "Into the night. Through
death. Behind, there gleams the morning dawn."

At the beginning of the third act we find Brand and
Agnes, with their baby boy, living on the margin of the
sunless fiord under the overhanging rock, and we learn
something of the progress of his work. He is still true
to his old motto, "everything or nothing." His uncompromising devotion and his overmastering individuality have produced a profound impression in

his parish. The commonplace, material, matter-of-
fact tradition of the place, impersonated in the bailiff
of the town, though not overcome, is forced into a
kind of acquiescence in his leadership, and a new spirit
seems to be abroad. And Brand himself is in one
sense changed. Till now no strong human affection
has ever claimed him. In the home of his youth and
at school he was a stranger. A hideous act of
covetous heartlessness, of which he was an unsuspected
witness, completely alienated him from his mother
when he was yet a child. The grandeur and heroism
of his character had been untempered hitherto by the
personal tenderness the whole wealth of which he now
pours out for his wife and child. But Agnes com-
plains that to others his love is still hard, and that in
the terrible sternness of his demand, "all or nothing,"
he repels instead of winning. His old mother yearns
with a superstitious longing to receive the sacrament
and the assurance of forgiveness from him on her
deathbed. He lays down the condition that before
she dies she shall give away the whole of that wealth
for which she has sinned, and toiled, and pinched, and
lived a loveless and sunless life, and shall go naked
into her grave. In vain she pleads that he is bidding
her scatter her very soul to the winds. He is inexorable. In the anguish of a deathbed repentance she
sends messengers to him. She offers half her wealth,
at last nine-tenths of it ; but is only met with the old
answer, "everything or nothing," and dies muttering,
" God is not so hard as my son," comforted, so says
the almost broken-hearted Brand, by the old lie, look-

ing upon God, as all the rest do, as a good-natured
huckster that may be beaten down if he cannot get
his full price. And yet this man, now that his love is
awakened, is visited in spite of himself by seasons of
compunction if not of doubt. To stand before men
with his awful "everything or nothing" draws tears of
blood from his heart. In loneliness he bites the
tongue with which he has chastised, and when he lifts
his arm to strike, the passionate longing comes over
him to embrace the weak and sinful brother.

Then comes his own trial. He and Agnes both
notice, though neither will confess it, the pale cheek
and waning strength of their boy. Surely, says Brand,
God cannot take him from them. Yet what if he can?
May not God do to-day what "the terror of Isaac"
did long ago? Then comes the doctor's verdict. It
is certain death to the child to stay another month on
the sunless fiord, and Brand in an agony of appre-
hension orders immediate preparations to be made
for leaving their home that very hour.

Then one after another, from the mouth of the
doctor himself, from the parishioner who has heard a
report that he means to leave them on receiving his
inheritance from his mother, from the poor mad girl,
Gerd, who is so strangely connected with his fate,
from every side come echoes of his own teaching, "all
or nothing." He has given up his ambition, he has
given up his life to his work in his remote parish, he
has refused to yield or to depart, has nailed his flag to
the mast and declared that here he will stand or fall
in conflict with his foe. He has given much for his

work on the fiord. Yet it is nothing if he will not
give all. Now he realises what he has been demanding
of others, and stands horror-smitten before his own
motto, "all or nothing." Nominally he throws the
choice upon Agnes, but not till he has shown her that
there is no choice at all. Brand's awful God seems to
pass by in the thick darkness before our very eyes as
Agnes lifts her child on high and cries—

"God! the sacrifice thou can'st demand I can lift up
towards thy heaven! Guide me through life's horror!"

When next we see Brand and his wife their child
has been lying for months beneath the sod of the
churchyard. It is Christmas-eve, the children's
festival. Brand is not content with having made the
sacrifice; he demands that there shall be no repining,
no tender idolatries, no cherished memories making
the season of rejoicing into a season of mourning.
Agnes must not dwell on the contrast between this
Christmas and the last; she must not draw the curtain
back that the light may stream upon the little grave;
she must not even plead for time and beg her husband
to have patience with her. And at last when a wild
gypsy woman, with her mouth full of profanity and her
heart full of defiance, bursts into the house and begs
or rather demands the little garments that Agnes keeps
as sacred relics, that she may wrap them round her
own child born among curses and, as it were, baptised
in gin, she must part with all her treasure, must not
retain even a single relic—"all or nothing." Agnes

has at one point rebelled like a wild thing driven to
bay; but now a serene and perfect joy overspreads
her countenance, now she is free and triumphant, but
as she turns to her husband and thanks him for the
strength with which he has uplifted her, and for the
awful but now glorious vision of God that he has revealed to her, she bids him remember the old word,
"He who sees Jehovah dies."

Then there sweeps upon Brand the vision of his lonely
life and strife when Agnes shall be gone, and he folds
round her the arms of a giant and declares that she
shall not be taken from him. Nor need she be taken.
She tells him that if he will sink her down again into
the life from which he raised her, if he will hide from
her once more the God that he has revealed, if he will
bid her return to her idol-house and forget his "all or
nothing," she will have no power against him as he
unteaches any more than she had as he taught. Then
she can live and be his wife. But to see Jehovah is to
die; and unless he takes her back she must pass on
and leave him to fight alone.

"Soul!" cries Brand, "be steadfast to the last. 'Tis
victory's victory to forfeit all. The sum of loss has framed
thy gain, only the lost is our own for ever!"

Agnes used to say that the "church was too small,"
but she could give no account of what she meant by
it. The truth was that the church with its associations
and forms and traditions oppressed her; and the feeling
of narrowness and oppression translated itself into a

sense of physical confinement. Everything else was too big for her, she sometimes felt. Her husband, his vocation, his purposes, his presence, his will, his ways; the mountain that overhung her, the fiord that locked her in, her sorrows, her memories, her darkness, her strife, all were too big for her, only the church was too small.

The mad Gerd said the same. The church down there in the valley was poor and hideous because it was so small. She knew of a church up on the mountain height, a church of ice and rock, and snow, where waterfall and avalanche read the mass, and the wind preached amongst the snow-peaks.

And Brand himself felt that the ruinous and mouldering edifice, with its cramped and narrow walls, was the symbol of the pining and paltry spirit of a religion in its second childhood. He would dedicate his mother's wealth to the rearing of a church worthy of the religion he preached. It should be the symbol of a wider and a stronger faith in which life should find its unity. Its vault should stretch not only over faith and doctrine, but over all to which God has given the right to be in human life—the day's toil, the evening's rest, the cares of night, the fresh delight of childhood—all that can claim a lodgment in a human heart. The river that foams down its course, the waterfall that roars through the cleft, the voice from the storm's great lungs and the sounds that ring from the sea soul-caught should melt into one with the organ notes and the stave on the people's tongue !

So Brand builds his church-symbol. And from all around the people stream to fill the air with commonplace laudations of his generosity, to give him knowing advice as to the best way of turning his gift to the advantage of the State—and his own; to burn in upon his tortured soul the fact that of all his deeds this one is least understood; to madden him by showing him that his symbol has none but a material meaning for the world; to drive him to fanaticism when he sees that all he does or says feeds the very spirit of commonplace against which he is fighting; to teach him that his church itself has become one huge lie and that its dedication will be his lying reward.

Overladen now with his sorrow and his defeat, and losing all touch with practical reality, goaded yet further on the path he has been taking, and no longer recognising any physical limitations or conditions of his mission, he turns the key contemptuously in the lock of the church door and flings it into the river, and summoning the people to follow him on his crusade through the world, and show that "life" and "God's service" are one, he leads the multitude up on to wild mountain heights whither they follow him in the belief that he is an inspired prophet and can work miracles for their sustenance and glory. When, hungry and footsore, they halt, and learn, in answer to their demand, that they must look for life-long toil, must strip themselves naked of every joy and comfort, that a crown of thorns pressed upon every brow will be their wages, and a free soul their reward, they

turn round fiercely upon the "deceiver" and chase
him with blows and curses out into the snow-fields.

Weary, bleeding, and alone, Brand now sees as in
vision the people for whom he has sacrificed himself,
the God whom he has striven to serve, the home and
happiness that he has lost.

Those miserable thralls, whom he has given his very
life to raise out of their sordid cares, will sink lower
and lower. Their national history passes before him.
He sees them sheltering their cowardice under the
plea of feebleness, sitting still while their brethren in
Denmark are crushed; bribed by English gold to
polute their land with smoke and their hearts with
greed; drawing aside from the great spiritual battles
of the world, suffering the old faith to die, and taking
no part in establishing the new; for their stake in the
world's redemption is too small to fight for. Not for
them was the cup drained, not for them did the crown
of thorns strike its teeth into the Saviour's temples,
not for them the thrust of the Roman lance into his
side, not for them the burning of the nails that
pierced his hands and feet, not for them the bearing
of the cross—the purple ridge that rose upon his
shoulder under the leather thong with which the
cobbler Ahasuerus smote him, is Norway's "fraction
of the passion." These are the men he, Brand, had
sought to redeem!

And as for the God whom he had striven to bring
men to serve with whole heart, had he not accepted
his all and then rejected him? Had he not quenched
every light that shone upon his path, had he not

suffered him to be crushed in utter defeat, had he not
flung back his prayers to him and deserted him in his
utmost need?

Through the storm he hears the sentence of doom
chanted,

Never, never can'st be like him, for in flesh hast
thou been made. Do his bidding or desert him, either
way alike thou'rt lost! Worm, thou never can'st be like
him, though thou drain the cup of death! Follow
after or desert him, either way thy deeds are doomed.
Dreamer! ne'er shalt thou be like him; lands and goods
though thou hast lost; all thou giv'st can naught enrich
him—for the earth-life wast thou formed.

And in the service of this inexorable and unapproachable God, for the sake of these sordid and
unredeemable earthlings, what had he lost? Agnes
and his baby boy might yet have been his—may yet
be his, for Agnes appears to him, in his fever, and
tells him that all the loss and sorrow is but a dream.
She is still living, and so is their boy. They may
have peace and joy if he will but strike a line through
these three words, "everything or nothing," and fall
into the even easy ways against which he has fought
in vain. No, never! If indeed it has been a dream,
then he will now make that dream a reality, will lose
wife and child and everything sooner than endure the
devil's breath of compromise! Whereat the shadowy
form of the tempter vanishes with a shriek, " Then
die! The world has no use for thee."

Then comes the end. From the mad Gerd he

learns more than the wisdom of the wise had taught him. He learns in penitential tears that while the name of Jesus has been on his lips, he has never been bathed in his spirit, that while proudly thinking himself another Saviour by whose wounds the world may be healed, he has not even found salvation for his own poor soul.

With still unbroken will, recognising himself as the poorest thing that creeps the earth, feeling that he stands on the lowest round of the ladder, yet still with fresh hope as the new truth breaks upon him, Brand rises to begin his journey anew.

But his weary and shattered powers are spared the fresh trial. For Gerd brings down an avalanche by a rifle shot, and as the great snow-slip sweeps over him and her, Brand cries to God from the jaws of death to answer whether man's modicum of *will* weighs a single grain in the scales of salvation. And as the crashing of screes and ice overwhelms him and fills the valley, a voice thunders the answer, " He is the God of Love."

It is impossible to read Brand, especially in the light of Ibsen's previous poems and experiences, without perceiving that his feelings towards his country-men are accurately reflected in Brand's withering denunciations. But it is likewise impossible not to perceive that he is conscious throughout that Brand is treading a path that leads to no goal. Though his character is sketched with a sympathy that sweeps us with it, yet we see from first to last that he is essentially a fanatic, that his formula, " everything or nothing," is one by which man cannot live, and that

his aimless crusade in the snow-fields is the legitimate
outcome of his principles. If human ties are in truth
to go for "nothing," if starvation on the one hand
and material improvements and prosperity on the
other are to go for "nothing," then the very harmony
which Brand seeks becomes impossible. "Your
idea," says one of his opponents, "seems to be to
combine God's service with potato planting; and you
go on as if God himself were aboard every fishing
smack," and Brand accepts this account of his pro-
posed reformation. But potatoes and fishes clearly
are not "everything." It should follow, then, that
they are "nothing," and if so why should we have
potato plots and fishing smacks at all? Brand is
driven step by step practically to admit that we
must not.

And yet if we decline to follow him we seem to fall
back into the miserable, paltry spirit of compromise
against which he protests. Is the conclusion, then,
that the requirements of this life are hopelessly irrecon-
cilable with high faith and lofty principle, and that
men must choose between being sordidly practical
and nobly fanatical? Or had Brand in some sense
wasted his heroism for want of the consecration of
sympathetic love?

If the concluding passage of the drama, in which
this latter answer seems to be given, stood alone, we
might hesitate to take it as Ibsen's deliberate teaching.
But it does not stand alone. A rapid review of
Brand's relations with five other characters in the play
will suffice to convince us of this. The good and

wise old doctor, whose pregnant words enforce the
lesson of Brand's experience, is sketched too slightly
to challenge further comment.

First, then, let us take the clerical dignitary who
pursues his successful way through his ecclesiastical
career without earnestness, without consecration, without soul. With the shallow and unspiritual shrewdness
of worldly wisdom ; with the vanity that often besets
successful performers—whatever their stage ; with a
soul-destroying familiarity with sacred themes unaccom-
panied either by depth of feeling or by conscious
insincerity ; never entertaining a doubt as to the
importance of his office or the truth of his teaching,
but not knowing what consecration or faith means, the
arch-deacon steadily pursues his own advancement
and cannot comprehend what Brand is aiming at if
he is not doing the same. And when Brand, mad-
dened by his sordid counsels, turns upon him and
cries, "Aye, fear of punishment and hope of gain is
the Cain-mark upon thy brow ! It cries aloud that in
thy worldly wisdom thou hast slain thy heart's pure
Abel !" he is so far from understanding him that he
is shocked and offended at being addressed by the
familiar "thou," and pays no attention at all to the
substance of the remark.

With such a man we can well forgive Brand for
breaking off all relations. He could but live his own
life independently of him. His very breath was
poison. But we also have the bailiff of the town, a
man whom Brand himself recognises as well-meaning,
honest, and, after his own fashion, industrious, warm,

and just. The material welfare and the decorous
government of the place are the constant subjects of
his thoughts and schemings. It is true that he has no
breadth of view, no poetry, and indeed no soul, except
officially. But that he had a soul officially is testified
by the fact that he contemptuously refused to save it
at the expense of the archives, for which he was
officially responsible, and which were threatened by a
fire. "Oh, save your soul!" cried his poor wife in an
agony of fear. "My soul!" he answered, "the Devil
take my soul! Help me to get out the archives!"
This man, with his limited ideas, who strove to do his
duty—but always within his own district;—who had
his share of personal ambition, and who looked for
some reasonable reward for his untiring devotion to
duty could not, of course, understand Brand in the
least; but Brand might have understood him, respected
him, worked with him, and ultimately even taught him
something. Instead of this he looks upon him as the
most deadly foe of his work. The things the bailiff
busies himself with are not "everything"—then they
must be "nothing." Because he minds material, and
not spiritual things, he is a scourge to his land. Earth-
quakes, flood, and winter-blast, famine, frost, and
pestilence, work less havoc than he from year to year;
for they can only rob the life, but he! how many
thoughts he cleaves, how many wills he deadens, how
many a song he chokes; how many a smile on the
people's lips, how many a flash in the people's bosom,
how many a thrill of exalting joy or wrath that might
have grown into a deed, has such a narrow and

material soul laid in a bloodless grave! And so it is
war between Brand and the bailiff, war in which Brand
appears to be completely victorious and his foe appears
to become his disciple, and honestly means to be so;
but he has understood nothing and learned nothing;
he has lost his dignity and self-respect, he has swallowed
his principles, and at last he has stooped to unworthy
means of retaining or regaining his influence. All
that Brand has done is to degrade an honest and
patriotic man.

Agnes he does not degrade. But he tortures her
to death. The love that she has taught him to feel
he dare not trust, in his dealings with others, lest it
should soften the sternness of his awful gospel.

No word is soiled with lies like that word "love."
Under its veil, with Satan's guile, men hide their want
of will, treacherously skinning over a life of dallying.
Is the way narrow, toilsome, steep? Oh, cut it short—
in "love!" Does one tread the broad path of sin? Yet
is there hope for him—in "love." Seeing his goal, does
he shrink back from the strife? He may still be victorious—in "love." Does he choose the wrong although
he knows the right? There is a refuge still—in "love."

God's love is not such. His love is hard even to
the horror of death; it bids our caresses wound like
blows; it let Jesus pray and pray in sweat and anguish,
"take this cup away," and then made him drink it to
the dregs. The God men worship now-a-days would
have shown his love by proclaiming a reprieve at the

foot of the cross, and conducting the work of redemption by a diplomatic correspondence!

So even when Brand feels sympathy he does not show it, and so he lacks the tenderness that alone can enable men to understand and guide their fellows. And therefore when he rightly seeks to wean Agnes from her tender idolatries, and when she herself longs for his support and guidance, he has nothing but words of stern rebuke for the "sorrows and memories and flood of sinful longings," that possess her, and he tears down her idol-temple with so hard a hand that she must die. Feeling the heroic grandeur of her husband's character in contrast with the pusillanimity of those around him, feeling that he is bound by his own life principle, and must not shrink from bearing what he did not shrink from inflicting, with her protests overborne and her instincts trampled upon as sinful, with her deep-seated love and loyalty recognising in her very tortures a higher life than she had ever known in her light-hearted joy, Agnes rises to the height of her husband's heroism, though she can not bring him to the purity and truth of her own insight. She seizes the heart of truth in his false-true gospel, suppresses her own rebellious protest,—and dies.

Yet another, and in some ways the most striking condemnation of Brand's motto, is furnished by one of those apparently capricious and wanton scenes in which Ibsen not rarely hides his deepest teaching. Just before the expected consecration of the Church, (which, as we have seen, is the signal for Brand to break away from all practical restraint, and accept the ab-

solute fanaticism which is the only legitimate outcome
of his principle), Einar—Agnes's former lover—comes
upon the stage once more. Brand turns to him with
the passionate longing to find some man with a living
heart and soul amongst all the cautious, self-seeking,
commonplace materialists by whom he is surrounded.
But he finds the gay poet and artist changed indeed.
Since last they met he has fallen into dissipated ways,
been ill, lost his joy in life, become "converted," and
is now a revivalist of the vulgarest and most offensive
type. At first he shows no interest in his old love
whatever ; but presently recalls " the young female
who held him in the net of desire before he was
cleansed in the bath of faith." Yes, he would like to
know how it goes with her—but only the essential.
Brand tells him of her marriage, her wifehood, her
motherhood, her bereavement, and her death. But
what are all these mundane trivialities to the evangelist ? He wants to know the essential only. *How*
did she die ? " With hope in a coming dawn, with
the heart's rich treasure whole, with will unbroken
to the last, with thanksgiving for all that life had given
and taken away, she sank into her grave." Why waste
the evangelist's time with such stuff and nonsense ?
How did her faith stand ? " Unshaken." But on
whom ? " On God." What ! only on him ? Then
she's damned—more's the pity. And with a parting
shot at Brand as likely to share her fate the converted
sinner goes his way rejoicing that *he* is saved.

Here then is a man to whom his religion is " everything," and his love and his humanity " nothing." Is

this the whole and renovated man that God must recognise as his noblest work? Here is one who lives
and thrives in peace and satisfaction on Brand's
formula of "all or nothing." What does Brand think
of him? He is filled with loathing for the creature
that dares to utter his blasphemies against heaven and
the sainted dead, but he never suspects that he has
here before him the only possible realisation of his
own life-slaying principle. For Ibsen is relentless in
picturing the blindness that shuts men's eyes to every
warning when they have once taken and persisted in
the wrong road. He shews us how often the enlighten-
ment of such is impossible with man, and (like the
Greek tragedians) hints only in quasi-supernatural
scenes at the close that it is yet "possible with God."

Brand then does not see the meaning of Einar's
wretched existence. But surely we can. Only the
man whose heart is dead can live by that destroying
word "all or nothing." The principle which slays
the saintly Agnes and drives her heroic husband mad,
fits the miserable Einar like a glove; he is happy and
at home with it.

And lastly we return to the mad girl Gerd. She is
a kind of symbolic foreshadowing of what Brand himself must come to in the end. She shares his contempt of the stifling atmosphere of the valley down
by the fiord; she hates the mouldering little church;
she speaks, with him, of a nobler and diviner edifice
where there is safety from the haunting foe against
which she wages ceaseless war—but alas! the beauty
of her church is cold. It is the avalanche and land-

slip that read the mass in it; the preacher is the wind that blows over the snow-fields, whose preaching sends the burning and the chill through the worshipper, and the approach is marked by the whitening bones of the living things that it has slain.

Step by step, throughout the poem, Brand is unconsciously approaching this ice-church. When child and wife are gone, he still tries to make life one by the formula of elimination, not of harmony, "all or nothing." But he has already broken with all human affections, broken with all the practical conditions of life. No wonder that the church he has built appears to him only a compromise and a lie. Driven by a vague instinct to the full working out of his principle, he leads his would-be followers away from the scene of their daily toils, away from all means of livelihood, up to the sublime but barren heights of the snow-fields; rejects the devotion that offers much but shrinks from giving all; and at last discovers that the goal, to which he has been striving to lead them, and to which he has attained alone, is the ice-church where he is chilled to the bone, and feels himself a thousand miles from the light and peace for which he longs.

Then comes to him the vision of that love which he has quelled within his bosom, and he weeps the tears which to Gerd's inspired imagination melt the shroud of the snow-field, melt the surplice of the ice-priest, melt the ice in her own heart. "Man! Why wept you not before?"

And as the avalanche descends and the voice proclaims "He is the God of love," the ice-church seems to melt and thaw into Brand's ideal of a church as wide as the life of nature and of man, the church that they may yet build who, heroic as he, suffer their heroism to be warmed and guided by love.

LECTURE III.—"PEER GYNT."

"BRAND" was published in 1866, and in 1867 "Peer Gynt" followed. The fundamental themes and motives of the two works are the same, but in other respects they present a complete contrast. The solemnity and monotony of "Brand" yield to a dazzling variety and play of wit in "Peer Gynt." The reader is fairly bewildered on a first or second reading, and is unable to trace any leading purpose or connection running through the grotesque contrasts and wild fancies of the drama. But in reality it is a simpler work than "Brand." The machinery is immensely more complicated, but the unity of conception is completer. It would be a paradox to call "Peer Gynt" more compact than "Brand," but it would be a paradox containing an important truth.

In "Brand" the hero is an embodied protest against the poverty of spirit and half-heartedness that Ibsen rebelled against in his countrymen. In "Peer Gynt" the hero is himself the embodiment of that spirit. In "Brand" the fundamental antithesis, upon which, as its central theme, the drama is constructed, is the contrast between the spirit of compromise on the one

hand, and the motto " everything or nothing " on the
other. And " Peer Gynt " is the very incarnation of
a compromising dread of decisive committal to any
one course. In " Brand " the problem of self-realisation and the relation of the individual to his surroundings is obscurely struggling for recognition, and in
" Peer Gynt" it becomes the formal theme upon
which all the fantastic variations of the drama
are built-up. In both plays alike the problems of
heredity and the influence of early surroundings are
more than touched upon ; and both alike culminate
in the doctrine that the only redeeming power on earth
or in heaven is the power of love.

" Peer Gynt," as already stated, stands for the Norwegian people, much as they are sketched in " Brand,"
though with more brightness of colouring. Hence
his perpetual " hedging " and determination never so
to commit himself that he can not draw back. Hence
his fragmentary life of smatterings. Hence his perpetual brooding over the former grandeur of his family,
his idle dreams of the future, and his neglect of every
present duty. Hence his deep-rooted selfishness and
cynical indifference to all higher motives ; and hence,
above all, his sordid and superstitious religion ; for to
him religion is the apothesis of the art of " hedging."

But Ibsen's allegories are never stiffly or pedanti-
cally worked out. His characters, though typical, are
personal. We could read " Brand," and could feel
the tragedy and learn the lessons of the drama without
any knowledge whatever of the circumstances or feelings under which it was written, or the references to

the Norwegian character and conduct with which it teems.

So, too, with " Peer Gynt." We may forget the national significance of the sketch, except where special allusions recall it to our minds, and may think only of the universal problems with which the poem deals, and which will retain their awful interest when Ibsen's polemic against his countrymen has sunk into oblivion. The study of " Peer Gynt " as an occasional poem should be strictly subsidiary and introductory to its study as the tragedy of a lost soul.

What is it to be one's self? God *meant something* when he made each one of us. For a man to embody that meaning of God in his words and deeds, and so become in his degree a "word of God made flesh " is to be himself. But thus to be himself he must slay himself. That is to say, he must slay the craving to make himself the centre round which others revolve, and must strive to find his true orbit and swing, self-poised, round the great central light. But what if a poor devil can never puzzle out what on earth God *did* mean when he made him? Why, then, he must *feel* it. But how often your " feeling " misses fire! Aye! there you have it. The devil has no stauncher ally than *want of perception !*

But, after all, you may generally find out what God meant you for if you will face facts. It is easy to find a refuge from facts in lies, in self-deception, and in self-sufficiency. It is easy to take credit to yourself

for what circumstances have done for you, and lay
upon circumstances what you owe to yourself. It is
easy to think you are realising yourself by refusing to
become a "pack-horse for the weal and woe of others,"
keeping alternatives open and never closing a door
behind you, or burning your ships, and so always re-
maining the master of the situation and self-possessed.
If you choose to do these easy things you may always
"get round" your difficulties, but you will never get
through them. You will remain master of the situation indeed, but the situation will become poorer and
narrower every day. If you never commit yourself,
you never express yourself, and your self becomes less
and less significant and decisive. Calculating selfishness is the annihilation of self.

One of the most striking of the secondary characters
introduced into the play is a certain conscript peasant.
War has broken out and this peasant must serve in
the army. He can only escape by maiming himself,
and so branding himself with lasting shame and dis-
honour. But he is committed by character and
conduct to a life of peaceful industry. His relations
with the woman who has trusted him are such that to
leave her now would be to throw upon her the burden,
and even the shame, which he would escape. He
chooses to bear them himself; and Peer Gynt sees
him, when he thinks he is alone, deliberately chop off
a finger. Peer soliloquises, "One might think of it,
wish it, determine it even—but do it ! no, that I can't
understand." And for that very reason Peer never
became what the poor maimed peasant was—himself.

But it is high time for me to introduce the hero of whom I have already spoken so much.

Peer or Peter Gynt, then, is a young Norwegian peasant sprung of a once wealthy family, and haunted by dreams of future magnificence, but living with his widowed mother in poverty, which his lounging indolence only serves to aggravate. With more than a touch of poetry in his soul, but with the narrow horizon of a peasant, the wildest flights of his imagination always fettered by the scanty material of his mental furniture, and his imagined grandeur incongruously yoked with the coarseness and homeliness of the only experiences out of which he can build it, Peer Gynt always believes himself called to a greatness which he never does anything to attain. The scanty remnants of the family property go to ruin while Peer fights and drinks, hunts and lies, always telling his mother, Aase, she'll be proud of him yet, when he has done "something really grand," and is made emperor; while she is sometimes half-carried away by his tales, and sometimes limits her anticipations to a doubtful hope that he may some time "get so far as having wit enough to mend his own breeches." For this man who imagines himself the hero of all the traditional exploits on record, and in retelling them as fragments of his own biography "makes it all so wild and grand," weaves in such marvellous touches of poetry and spells of terror that his own mother hardly recognises the tales she has known from her childhood, and was herself maybe the first to tell her son; this man who regards himself as the natural superior of all around

him, and who demands their admiration and sub-
mission as his obvious due, is chiefly distinguishable
from his fellows, to the eye of sense, by his tattered
and disreputable exterior.

A single specimen of Peer's imaginary adventures
must suffice. He is lounging down a mountain path
with Aase.

Aase. Peer, you're lying.
Peer Gynt. No, I'm not.
Aase. Well, then, swear to it.
Peer Gynt. What should I swear for?
Aase. Pooh! you dare not. It's all stuff and non-
sense.
Peer Gynt. It's true ; every blessed word.
Aase. Aren't you ashamed to look in your mother's
face? First, you're off to the mountains, months
on end, in the thick of harvest, stalking deer on the
snow-fields ; then you come home with a tattered
coat, without rifle, and without game ; and then you try
to make me swallow all your monstrous hunter's lies !—
Well, then, where did you come upon the stag?
Peer Gynt. West by Gendin.
Aase. Yes, of course !
Peer Gynt. A sharp wind was blowing towards me.
Hidden behind a clump of trees, he was scraping for
lichen under the snow with his hoof.
Aase. Oh, yes, of course !
Peer Gynt. I held my breath, stood listening, heard
the crunching of his hoof, saw the branches of one of
his horns. Then cautiously I dragged myself forward
on my belly, and glanced up from my hiding-place
among the stones. Such a stag ! You never saw a
sleeker or fatter.

Aase. Just to think!

Peer Gynt. Bang went the gun, and the stag plunged down upon the slope. But at the very moment he fell, I leapt across his back, seized his left ear, and was just going to drive my knife into his neck behind his skull, when the beast leapt up with a wild shriek, struck knife and sheath out of my hand with a back cast, screwed me fast round the loins, pinned his horns against my calves, clipped me in a vice, and set out with a spring right over Gendin-edge.

Aase. In the name of Jesus!

Peer Gynt. Have you ever seen the Gendin-edge? It's good three miles in length, and as sharp as a scythe on the top. Right over glaciers, screes, and slopes, and grey boulder-stones, you can look plump down on either side into the lakes that slumber, dark and heavy, more than thirteen hundred fathoms below. Right along the edge he and I cleft the air on our way. Such a colt I ne'er bestrode before. . . Brown-backed eagles swam in the vast, dizzy cleft, halfway betwixt us and the waters, and dropped behind like motes. Ice-falls broke and crashed upon the strand, but we could hear no sound, only the sprites of the whirlwind leapt as in a dance,—sang and swung before our ears and eyes.

Aase. Oh, God help me!

Peer Gynt. All at once, just at a desperate precipice, a startled ptarmigan flashed, quacking, into the air, from the crag that hid him, bang in front of the stag's feet upon the edge. The stag swung half round, and set out with a leap to heaven, right into the deep with the two of us!

Behind the black mountain wall, beneath the bottomless abyss.

First we cleft a bank of clouds, then we cleft a flock of sea-gulls that flew shrieking to every side to escape us.

Down without rest or stay we went, but in the depth there glittered something whitish, like a reindeer's belly. Mother! it was our own reflection rising up through the silent mountain tarn to the crust of the water, in the same wild course with which we plunged downwards.

Aase. Peer! God help me. Tell me quick!

Peer Gynt. The stag from the clouds, and the stag from the bottom, butted together at the same moment, while the foam splashed round us. There we lay floundering. And in the long-run, you, we managed to get to land towards the north somehow. The stag swam, and I clung on to him. So then I came home.

Aase. But the stag, you?

Peer Gynt. Oh! he's there still, I suppose. [*Snaps his fingers and turns on his heel.*] If you can find him, you may have him.

The incongruity between Peer's pretensions and his appearance, and his measureless bragging and lying, make him the scorn and sport of the whole neighbourhood. He feels it cutting into his very heart, and though he thirsts for recognition and applause, yet he is never really happy except when alone, or when, to use his own quaint phraseology, he is "a bit lopsided" —*i.e.*, in liquor. For then the scorn "does not bite." At other times he perpetually hears the titter and marks the sidelong glances of his mockers, and ever and again the wild desire comes over him " to lay the grip of a butcher on their throats and tear the contempt out of their breasts." Then with burning cheek he will fling himself upon his back and gaze into the sky and float away into dreamland, tracing his own

form in some fantastic cloud, and seeing himself ride
in triumph over sea and land, while all the world gazes
on him in wonder, and " England's emperor and all
England's girls gather on the beach to do him honour."

He has a keen natural relish for social enjoyment,
in spite of his sensitiveness, and when he can forget
himself, that wonderful fascination which seems exclusively to pertain to natures at once indolent and
powerful asserts itself.   Naturally, his mother, though
she rates him soundly whenever she sees him, and is
always threatening dire vengeance on him for his
escapades, will not let any one else say a word against
her wonderful boy; and perhaps Ingrid, the only
daughter and heiress of the rich peasant at Haegstad,
is not the only girl to whom Peer Gynt would only
have to beckon if he wanted her.   In Ingrid's case,
family opposition would of course have to be reckoned
on, but then " the old man can never stand up against
his child.   He's obstinate enough in his way, but
Ingrid always comes over him in the end, and where-
ever she goes the old fellow comes, step by step,
hobbling and grumbling after her."   So says Aase,
when reproaching her ne'er-do-weel son for having lost
his chances.   It is too late now.   Ingrid is to marry
Mads Moen to-morrow.   This is news to Peer, who
has been no one knows where for six weeks or so,
and the name of that milksop Mads Moen in connection with a girl for whom he has himself perhaps had a
passing fancy, is too much for the future "emperor,"
and there and then he dashes off to put a stop to the
proceedings !

Haegstad is full of company. Dancing and singing are in full swing as Peer Gynt, forgetting his mission, and only longing to join in the frolic, leaps over the fence, glowing with animation, but is met with preconcerted contempt and indifference by all the girls and their partners.

At this moment Peer Gynt's good angel appears upon the scene. A family recently come from another neighbourhood joins the company. The decent and pious old couple come on together; and almost touching her mother's skirt, glancing down at her white apron and her shoes, with her psalm-book carefully wrapped in a cloth, after the fashion of Norwegian maidens on all occasions of state, comes Solvejg, hand in hand with her little sister Helga. She does not know Peer by sight, and is not in the conspiracy. She comes from another world, and brings another life with her. "It makes it Sunday to look at her." Here is Peer Gynt's "empire" if he is man enough to enter into possession of it. He may do so, for Solvejg's life is henceforth changed as well as his. Begotten of God in her virgin bosom at that first interview is an ideal Peer Gynt, such as God would have him be. This child of her own pure heart will grow till it becomes her very life, and, however sorely tried, she will never desert it or cease to believe that it exists.

Peer Gynt may ruin and annihilate his actual self; his ideal self is beyond even his own reach, safe in God's keeping and in hers. She at least knows *what God meant* when he made Peer Gynt.

When Solvejg hears her partner's name she hastily
withdraws her hand. She has just been forbidden by
her father to dance with him. Indeed, no one will
speak to him now save "the poor craven bridegroom,"
against whom in tearful disdain Ingrid has shut herself up in the storehouse, and who, vaguely believing
in Peer's remarkable powers, and very definitely conscious of his own entire helplessness, makes a whim-
pering appeal to him for assistance.

So now our hero stands definitely at the parting of
the ways. He may enter upon his true empire in
Solvejg's heart and life, and realise himself. But he
will have to work for that. A shorter cut, by which
he may escape from the contempt he cannot endure,
presents itself. A desperate act of self-assertion may
ruin his life and Ingrid's, but it will at least put him
henceforth beyond the reach of contempt.

First an unsuccessful attempt to frighten and bully
Solvejg; then one wild appeal, which comes too late,
for a prayer has no grace after a threat; and too soon,
for the new leaven of love has not yet worked in her
heart.

In a few moments confusion and amazement reign
at Haegstad. Peer Gynt is seen leaping up the
precipitous rocks like a goat, carrying off Ingrid to
the forest by a path on which no one who values his
neck cares to follow him.

So closes the first act of "Peer Gynt." The four
acts which follow show us how that true self-realisation
which was so near at hand and so easy to attain,
at least in its initial stages, on the dancing green at

Haegstad, fades away into the distance and becomes
ever harder and harder to recover, as self-assertion
and self-indulgence do their work.

The better self does not submit to its own destruction without a protest; nor does Solvejg's image fade
at once from her lover's heart. It is the vision of her
beauty and purity which makes poor Ingrid's reign so
short; yet when Ingrid is rejected, and returns to her
home, vowing vengeance, Peer yet further degrades
himself, still in mere loveless self-assertion, in coarse
amours with dissolute saeter girls. In moments of
physical depression and satiety he is visited, like other
sinners, with passing visions of nobler things:

There go two brown eagles sailing, and southward
the wild geese fly; and here in the mire knee-deep must
I tramp and moil. [*Leaps up.*] Yea! I will with them!
Yea! I will wash myself pure in the bath of the keenest
wind! I will up; I will plunge myself clean in the shining baptismal font. I will out o'er the saeter mountains;
I will ride me all sweet in soul.

But the new dreams of purity soon fade into the old
dreams of grandeur, and the downward course is still
pursued.

Then, more damning in some respects than his car-
nal sins—sins against purity, but not against love, for
there was not even unfaithful love in them—comes his
frivolous and burlesque courtship with the trold-
maiden, the daughter of the old man of the Dovre-
fjeld, and the love, so lightly bestowed and lightly

withdrawn, but indelible in its debasing influences,
which is to bring so fearful a retribution with it.

It is amongst the trolds that Peer finally learns
(while he believes himself to be rejecting) the art of
gaining and keeping self-respect by means of a self-
sufficiency that enables him to see all that is foul in
himself and his surroundings as though it were fair.
Thus he escapes from self-contempt and from the tor-
ture of his sensitiveness, but not by the only true path
—the path, namely, of self-discipline and self-realisation.

We must pass over the grim struggle with the invisible spirit—the sphinx-riddle of life, as is afterwards
hinted—that no man can grapple with or slay, that
crushes all individuality out of Peer Gynt, teaches him
the lesson of "going round" instead of "going through,"
and draws him inch by inch to spiritual self-oblitera-
tion.

Peer Gynt is now far gone on the way to perdition,
but the extremest consequences of his sins and weakness have for the present been warded off; for Solvejg
has been a kind of guardian angel to him, and the
powers of evil have been partially baulked by her influence and Aase's. These two have been much together, and Solvejg has gradually learned the whole
story of her lover's early life. Every hint has served
to strengthen the mysterious power which draws her
to him, and as long as her devotion follows him, sym-
bolised in the church-bells which ring at her bidding,
and break the trold charm that bound him, so long
may the dark powers be baffled in their last attempts ;

and Peer, on his side, though ever falling, still thinks
of Solvejg as the fairest and purest of earthly things,
still seeks occasion for sending her messages, and still
feels that if she does not forget him there is hope for
him yet.

Before his final apostasy the forces of good and evil
are to meet in open conflict. His ideal is to present
itself to him once more in its living warmth before it
fades away into a dim, half-forgotten tradition.

Peer Gynt is an outlaw—the penalty of the rape of
the bride—and it is at the peril of his life if he ven-
tures beyond the limit of the forest. He has built
himself a forest home with reindeer antlers over the
gable, and is making fast the great wooden lock when
Solvejg herself comes on her snow shoes over the
mountain stretches, obeying the mysterious impulse
which draws her to this man, her girlish bashfulness
yielding to a womanly faithfulness that can never be
broken, as with firm voice she says : [1]

God's blessing on thy toil! Thou must not reject me.
At thy summons I come, and thou must receive me.
   Peer. Solvejg ! It cannot be !—and you dare to ap-
proach me ?
   Solvejg. A summons thou sentest me by little Helga,
and in storm and in stillness there came many after it.
All the words of thy mother were nought but a summons.
A summons that teemed when the dreams came upon me.
By heavy night and empty day was the same summons
borne—that now I must come. It seemed as though life
were all stifled down there ; neither laughter nor tears

---

[1] I give the dialogue in a much contracted form.

could come straight from the heart. I knew not, indeed, what mind thou mightest cherish; but I knew and knew well what I should do and must. On my snow shoes I came. When I asked for the way, and they said, "Wherefore go'st thou?" I said, "'Tis my home!"

Peer. So then away with plank and with nail! What need of defence from the haunting sprites! Solvejg! Let me look at you—no, not too near! only look at you! Oh, but I will not smirch thee. With outstretched arms will I hold thee away, O thou beauteous and warm! Nay, who would have thought it, that I could so draw thee? But oh! I have longed for thee daytime and night. See here, I have timbered and built me a house, but down shall all come, 'tis too poor and too foul. My princess! Ay, now she is found and won; full soon shall the palace uprise from the rock!

Axe in hand, Peer strides to the forest, but there he is met by the trold-maid he had so lightly loved, become in a few months a leering old woman with a hideous imp, the offspring, by the weird law of troldland, of his wanton thoughts; for in that land thoughts shape themselves relentlessly into outward fact, and even the blindest is forced to see that they are indelible as deeds. The trold-maid and imp have come to claim him. Let him marry Solvejg to-morrow if he will, but they will come and demand their share. Where there is room for two there is room for three, and where Peer Gynt and Solvejg sit, there will the trold-woman find her way, and she and Solvejg will go turn and turn about with him!

er Gynt. There falls all my palace in ruins and

dust. A wall rises round her whom I was so near. All
the beauty is darkened and my joy is struck old. Go
round, lad! You can ne'er find a way through, across
this, to her from thyself. Through? Yet surely there
should be a way. There stands written a word, if I well
mind it, concerning repentance. But what? what is it?
I have not the book—have forgotten it most—and where
to get guidance out here in the forest? Repentance? It
might be whole years e'er I tore through that way.
'Twere a sorry life. To break up what is pure and beauteous and fair, and then tinker it up from the fragments
again? It may do with a fiddle, but not with a bell.
Where the grass shall grow green—why the feet must
ne'er trample. But it was a lie—her and her elfish snout.
Now the foul stuff is all out of sight. Yes! out of sight is
it, but not out of mind. Wriggling thoughts will follow
me in. Ingrid and those three [the saeter girls] that
came leaping over the hills, will they be there too? And
with taunt and leer will they claim like her to be taken to
my heart, to be lifted on tender and outstretched arms?
Go round it, lad; if my arms were as long as the pine-
tree's branch or the fir-tree's stem, I fear I should lift her
too near me still, to set her down stainless and unsmirched
again. I must get round this by what means I may, that
neither the gain may be mine nor the loss.—Shove it
away and forget it all! [*turns towards the house, but stops
short again*]. Go in after that, so befouled and ashamed?
Go in with all that trold-ship in train? Speak, yet be
silent; confess, yet conceal? 'Tis the Sabbath eve—to
go in and meet her, as I am now, were sacrilege.

Solvejg [*in the door*]. Are you coming?

Peer. Go round.

Solvejg. What?

Peer. You must wait; it is dark here, and I have a
heavy load.

Solvejg. Wait till I help you ; we'll share our burdens.
Peer. Nay, stay where you stand, I must bear it alone.
Solvejg. But it must not be long, you !
Peer. Be patient, girl.   Be the time long or short—you
must wait.
Solvejg [*nodding*]. Yes, wait !

> [Peer Gynt *crosses over into the forest ;*
>   Solvejg *is left standing in the half-*
>   *open door.*]

So Peer, seeing that his sins have cut him off from
immediate and painless entrance upon the possession
of his better self, instead of seeking to purify himself,
says that when a thing is broken it is too late to mend it,
and goes on, therefore, to break more things ; says
that where the ground is once trodden no green grass
can grow, and goes on to tread more places bare ; says
that he must bear the burden all alone, and so throws
it all upon Solvejg ; will not commit the sacrilege of
going into the home made bright by her presence,
and so makes all his after life a desecration of her
love.

He is equally selfish in his relations with the other
woman that loves him.   In the unrivalled pathos of
Aase's death-scene we see Peer at his best.   But in
his best is revealed his worst—his irredeemable
selfishness and shirking.

He has come to his mother for comfort, and she is
full of her own approaching death, the seizure of her
few properties in payment of Peer's fine for the rape

of the bride, and allusions to Solvejg's desertion of
her home for Peer's sake. There is little comfort
in these themes, and Peer will not have any of
them.

The scene opens with Aase lying alone in bed.
Her neighbour, Kari, has told her not to expect her
son to trouble himself about her, but she is certain he
will come.

Aase. O Lord, will he never come? Such a dreary
time I have waited. I've no one to send to fetch him,
and I've so much I want to say. There isn't a moment
to lose. So quickly! Who would have thought it!
Oh, if only poor Aase knew she hadn't been too hard
upon him!

Peer Gynt [*entering*]. Good-even!

Aase. God give you joy! So you've come then, my
dear, dear boy! But how dare you venture down here
where your life is in forfeit?

Peer Gynt. Oh, as to my life, it's all one. I couldn't
choose but come and see round.

Aase. Yes; now Kari will be put to shame; and I
can go off in peace!

Peer Gynt. Go off? What jabber is that? Why,
where do you want to go?

Aase. Ah, Peer, the end is coming; I haven't much
time left now.

Peer Gynt [*with an impatient swing, as he crosses the
floor*]. Look at that! When I'm trying to get out of
the worry, and thought I should be quit of it here!—Are
you cold in your hands and feet?

Aase. Yes, Peer. It will soon be over. When you

see my eyes glazing you must close them carefully to.
And then you must see to the coffin ; and be sure it's a
fine one, dear.—Oh, no, I forgot.

Peer Gynt. Oh, shut up with that ! There's time
enough yet.

Aase. Yes, yes. [*Looks uneasily round the room.*]
You see the poor sticks they've left me. Just like them !

Peer Gynt [*with a lurch*]. There again ! [*In a hard
voice.*] Of course it's all my fault. But what's the use
of casting it up at me ?

Aase. *Your* fault ! No, it was the cursed drink that
all the mischief came from ! My poor boy, you were
drunk, and we don't know what we're doing then, do we ?
And so you rode on the stag ! Yes, yes, right enough ;
you were dazed.

Peer Gynt. Just let that tale drop, mother. There ;
let the whole thing be ! We'll put off all the worries till
afterwards—till another time. [*Sitting on the side of the
bed.*] Now, mother, let's chat together, but only of odds
and ends, and forget all that's bitter and crooked, and all
that is sore and sharp. No ; look now ! Why, sure
enough, there's the old cat ! He's alive yet, I see !

Aase. Oh, he goes on at night so ! You know what
that means, you do.

Peer Gynt [*turning it off*]. What's the news in the
place here ?

Aase [*with a knowing smile*]. They say there's a
girl somewhere, yearning for the mountains.

Peer Gynt [*hastily*]. And Mads Moen—is he satis-
fied ?

Aase [*continuing*]. They say she's deaf to the two
old folks with their tears. *You'd* better go round and
call in there ; maybe *you* could do something, Peer.

Peer Gynt. But the smith, where has he come to
harbour ?

Aase. We won't talk of the filthy smith. I'd sooner tell you her name, lad; the name of the girl, you know.

Peer Gynt. Nay, now let us chat together, but only of odds and ends, and forget all that's bitter and crooked, and all that is sore and sharp. Are you thirsty? Shall I get you some drink? Can you stretch? The bed is full short. Let me see—why, don't I believe it's the crib that I had as a boy! Do you mind how oft of an evening you sat by my bed and spread the skins over me and sang and crooned me your songs?

Aase. Yes! don't you mind it—how we played sledges when your father was off on his journeys? The coverlet skin was the sledge-rug and the floor was a frozen fiord.

Peer Gynt. Yes; but the best of it all, mother, can't you remember that too? It was the gallant steed.

Aase. Yes, yes; do you think I don't know? It was Kari's cat we borrowed. He'd sit on the old wooden chair.

Peer Gynt. To the castle west of the moon, to the castle east of the sun, to Soria-Moria castle, the way ran high and low. A stick that we found in the cupboard you took for whip handle.

Aase. How I perked myself there on the cushions!

Peer Gynt. Yes, yes, and with loosened rein, you turned yourself round as we travelled to ask me if I was cold. God bless you, you ugly old darling, for you were a tender soul. Why, what are you groaning about?

Aase. My back! The hard boards hurt it so.

Peer Gynt. Stretch yourself out, I'll support you. So, so, now you're lying at ease.

Aase [*uneasily*]. No, Peer, I must flit!

Peer Gynt. You must flit?

Aase. Yes, flit! That's what I keep wanting.

Peer Gynt. Oh, nonsense ! Spread the rug over you and let me sit down by the foot-board. See now, we'll shorten the hours by singing and crooning songs.

Aase. No ! better fetch the Good Book from the cupboard. I'm so troubled in my mind.

Peer Gynt. In Soria-Moria castle there is feasting for king and prince. You lie back upon the sledge cushions, and I'll drive you there over the downs.

Aase. But, Peer, dear, am I bidden ?

Peer Gynt. Yes ! that we are, both the two. [*Throws a string round the chair the cat is lying on, takes a stick in his hand and seats himself on the foot-board.*] Now speed thee, my Blackie, now speed thee— Mother, you're not too cold ? Aye, aye, you can tell by the gallop when Blackie is on the way !

Aase. Peer, dear, what is it ringing ?

Peer Gynt. The glittering sledge-bells, mother.

Aase. Hu ! what a hollow clanging !

Peer Gynt. We're driving over a fiord.

Aase. I'm scared by the rushing and sighing so strange and so wild in my ears !

Peer Gynt. It's the pine trees, mother. They're soughing out over the downs as we pass. Only lie still.

Aase. There's a glitter and gleaming out there afar. What does it come from, the shining ?

Peer Gynt. From the castle's windows and doors. Can you hear how they're dancing ?

Aase. Yes.

Peer Gynt. Outside is St. Peter standing and bidding you walk in, mother.

Aase. Does he greet me?

Peer Gynt. Yes, with all honour. And he pours out the sweetest wine.

Aase. Wine ? Has he cakes as well, then ?

Peer Gynt. I should think **so** ! A dish cram **full.** And the late arch-deacon's **lady is getting the coffee and meat.**

Aase. Oh, mercy ! then, shall I meet her ?

Peer Gynt. As often and snug **as you** please.

Aase. No ! think, Peer, to what a rejoicing you're driving poor **Aase** in.

Peer Gynt [*cracking his whip*]. Hie ! speed thee, my Blackie, now **speed thee.**

Aase. Peer, dear, **you're** driving right ?

Peer Gynt [*cracking his whip again*]. We're on the high road.

Aase. The journey has made me so weak and faint.

Peer Gynt. Now the castle rises before us, and **soon** will the journey be done.

Aase. I will lie back and shut my eyes, then, and leave all to you, **my boy.**

Peer Gynt. Now, speed thee, my Blackie, my charger. In the castle is bustle and stir ; they crowd and they swarm round the portals. And here come Peer **Gynt** and his mother ! **What say** you now, Mr. Saint Peter? Won't you let mother in ? I think you may search **far** and wide, sir, e'er you find me an honester **skin** ! Of myself I have little to say, I can turn me back from the portal. If you give me a drink I'll say thank you. If you don't, I shall never complain. [*Here some apparent reluctance on the part of the porter is at once quashea by an appeal to the supreme authority.*] Aye, didn't I know it ; I tell you ! [*To St. Peter.*] Now you'll dance to another tune ! [*Anxiously.*] Why does your eye seem glazing ? Mother ! Are you gone off your head ? [*Goes up to the bed-head.*] You mustn't lie there all staring ! Speak, mother ; it's me, your boy ! [*Feels her brow and* *hands tenderly; then throws the string over the chair, and in a low voice says—*] So, then, you may **rest now,** Blackie. We've come to the journey's end. [*Closes her eyes, and bows down over her.*] **Have** thanks for **each** day that **thou lived'st;** for *spank* and **for** *lullaby!* But now you must **thank me back,** mother. [*Presses his cheek against her mouth.*] **See there!** It was thanks **for the** lift.

On Aase's death Peer **leaves the** country, and we **catch** nothing **but a few** retrospective glimpses of his **subsequent adventures up to** middle life; for **when next we meet him he is a** wealthy **man of** fashion **surrounded by a chorus of** sycophants gathered from all nations, **to** dance, **as he** tells them in a moment of vinous **candour, round** his altar **of** the golden calf.

He **is still the same** man, **but** years of "hedging," **of** self-sufficiency, and of lying, have carried him much further forward **on the path of** insignificance, and his Norwegian glow and colouring have faded away. **He is a** commonplace, undistinguished, cosmopolitan **sinner,** material, worldly-minded, **and** cynical. He has picked up **a great deal** besides **gold** since last we saw **him, and it is his** boast that **he** has remained **himself** through all his changes **of** fortune. He has **got his** luck from America, his books **from** Germany, **his** waistcoat **and** his manners **from** France, his industry **and** keen eye for the main **chance** from England, his patience from the Jews, and **a** touch of the *dolce far niente* from Italy. On his education he **shall speak** for himself:

I am, as I have mentioned to you before, entirely self-taught. I have never studied anything methodically; but I have thought and speculated, and got up a little of everything. I began in advanced age, and you know it's rather hard work then to plough up and down the pages and push along through thick and thin. History I've taken in detachments. And since, in seasons of depression, one needs something firm to rest upon, I've taken religion—scrapwise. I think that's the way to make it run. One shouldn't read just for the sake of devouring, but to see what one can make available.

The most wonderful thing about this man now is his religion. It is quite of the type satirised in "Brand," only Peer Gynt has a strange gift of cynical frankness, rising to the point of genius, which enables him fluently and with shameless self-satisfaction to lay bare in his own mind the workings of a base and self-seeking religion, which other men live by but seldom openly profess. To borrow a witticism from another quarter, his religion is simply and solely an "insurance against fire." It sets the crown upon his systematic hedging operations. He made his money in the slave trade, and by exporting idols to China. He had religious scruples against both—especially the trade in idols. So he quieted his conscience by opening up another branch of trade with China, which consisted in equipping missionaries with Bibles and rum—at a profit. Things balanced in this fashion, he began after a time to feel uncomfortable about the slave trade. The philanthropic army was becoming formidable, and the risks were great; after all it was hardly a suitable trade "for one advanced in life." So his moral feeling triumphed. He gave up the trade, kept the last cargo for himself, turned planter, had his negroes religiously and morally instructed (which turned out a very good speculation), and when finally he sold the whole con-cern, he gave out grog all round gratis, so that every man and woman on the place had a spree. On the whole, then, he hopes that his sins are more than balanced, and that his account stands well with heaven.

But the most remarkable of his religious utterances I must give at length, once more premising that he *says* what many another man seems to believe, but what perhaps was never uttered by human tongue before and never will be again !

While he is asleep in a hammock on the coast of Morocco, his treacherous friends seize his yacht, with his treasure on board, and he wakes to see her putting out at full steam to sea.

Nightmare ! Nonsense ! I shall wake up soon ! She's off to sea, and at tearing speed. All nonsense ! I'm dreaming, I'm drunk, and daft ! Oh, surely it's impossible that I'm to die ! A dream ? Yes ! it *shall* be a dream. Frightful ! Alas ! it's all true ! My beasts of friends ! Oh, hear me, Lord God. Thou art so wise and so righteous ! O Judgment ! It's me—Peer Gynt ! O Lord God, think on me. Protect me, O Father ; else I am undone ! Make them reverse the engines. Make them lower the gig. Stop the thieves ; entangle the rigging somewhere. Listen to me. Let other folks' business alone. The world will shift for itself for a bit—No, by God he's not listening ! He's deaf as usual. A pretty state of things indeed. A God that can't help a fellow out of a fix like this [*with a gesture towards heaven*]. Wsh ! Haven't I given up the plantations and negroes ? Haven't I sent missionaries over to Asia ? One good turn deserves another ! Get me on board ! [*A flash shoots from the yacht and a thick cloud rolls up, a hollow sound booms. Peer Gynt utters a shriek and sinks upon the sand. Little by little the smoke clears away. The ship has disappeared.*]

Peer Gynt [*pale and with hushed voice*]. That was the sword of vengeance ! Gone down, man and mouse, in a moment. Blessings for ever on the stroke of chance— of chance ? No, it was more than that. I was to be delivered and they destroyed. Oh, thanks and praise that Thou hast protected me, that Thine eye was upon me, despite all my sins.—What a wonderful sense of security and trust there is in knowing oneself to be individually protected.—But in the desert ? How shall I get food and drink ? Oh, I shall find something. It's His business to see to that ! There's no such great danger. [*Insinuatingly.*] Oh, it isn't His will that I, a poor little sparrow, shall fall. Only let me be humble, and give Him His time. Let the Lord rule. Don't be downcast.— Was that a lion roaring in the reeds ? No, it wasn't a lion ! A lion ? Yes, certainly ! The beast, he'll take care to keep his distance. It isn't so easy to fight with your masters. They know that by instinct. . . . . But all the same, I should like to get up a tree. There are some acacias and palms waving over there. If I can get up I shall feel safe and sheltered—especially if I can remember a few psalms as well. [*Gets up and settles himself.*] How delightful to feel one's spirit exalted. Noble

thoughts are better than wealth. Only build upon Him.
He knows what measure of the cup of affliction I am man
enough to drink. He feels like a father towards me, in
person. [*Looking ruefully over the sea, where his yacht
and treasure have sunk.*] But economical?—No! *That*
he isn't.

The miscellaneous and somewhat disconnected
adventures that follow show us Peer Gynt in a variety
of characters, such as a company promoter interested
in developing the Sahara as an inland sea, a travelling
scholar and historian, and above all, a prophet in an
Arab community. It is in this last capacity that he
sinks lowest of all. He is disposed "graciously to fool"
Anitra, the chieftain's daughter, but owing to his im-
penetrable self-sufficiency she is able to fool him with
such completeness that even he for a moment con-
fesses himself "plucked and feathered," as Anitra
gallops off with his jewels and his purse, and leaves
him in the middle of the desert.

A few hours suffice to restore him, however, and in
the alchemy of his memory, the whole adventure
becomes a touching and noble "renunciation of the
joys of love" on his part for the disinterested pursuit
of truth.

And thus at each step he washes himself out more
and more completely, while boasting that he is still
"himself"; and becomes more and more convinced
of his own virtue as his moral nature goes more and
more completely to ruin.

When we have conducted him to his lowest depth

of insignificance, all the powers of earth, heaven, and hell seem to concentrate themselves upon showing him what he is, and in what sense his boast is true that he is " himself."

For instance, in Cairo he is taken into a madhouse by the doctor who has himself gone mad, without any one yet knowing it ; and on the strength of his declaration that he has always been " himself," he is proclaimed emperor of the madmen. Peer objects that the very thing about madmen is that they are " not themselves," to which the doctor answers :

Not themselves?   Now there you're profoundly mistaken ! Here, I assure you, people are most damnably themselves.   Themselves and not a jot besides ! Here they all go at full sail as themselves.   Each one shuts himself up in the cask of self, plunges deep down in the ferment of self. He's hermetically sealed with the bung of self, and he tightens the staves in the wells of self. None has a tear for another's woes, none has sense for another's ideas.   Ourselves—that's what we are in thought and in speech ; ourselves to outmost plank of the springboard.   And so if an emperor is to reign, it's clear that you're the appointed man.

Clear, indeed ! This is the way in which Peer has been himself.

I will not go through the gruesome scenes in the madhouse. They are all but lost on Peer. Now and again, just for a moment, the meaning of it all seems to hover before him.   " Mad and sane are the same misprint, " he exclaims bitterly ; but the vision, if it

comes near him, does not really touch him, and he
goes out of the madhouse sickened and horrified, but
not converted.

In the midst of his sins and selfishness we are
carried back for a moment to Norway, and hear
Solvejg's song :

Maybe there will pass both winter and spring, and the
next summer too, and the whole long year ; but at last
thou wilt come, I know it for truth, and I will still wait,
as I promised of yore.   God strengthen thee whereso
thou goest on earth : God gladden thee if now by His foot-
stool thou standest.   Here shall I wait till thou comest
again ; or, if thou waitest there, there meet we, beloved.

At last, after many wanderings and many changes
of fortune, Peer Gynt, an old man with the lines of
selfishness drawn yet harder upon his face, and certain
added traits of unloveliness conspicuous in his character, turns his face to Norway.   We must travel with
seven-leagued boots past the storm which throws him
penniless upon his native shore ; past the mysterious
and ghastly interview with the impersonation of
physical death and its terrors, which repels Peer Gynt,
but without wholesomely disturbing his self-sufficiency ;
past the revisiting of his old home, where he finds his
past history already a popular myth ; past his reflec-
tions on all the parts he has played during his life ; past
his obstinate self-sufficiency and now almost fiendish
selfishness.   Everything and everyone holds up to him
the mirror that he may see what he has become, but,

while shocked at the features he beholds, he never recognises them as his own.

At last, in his wanderings he comes to the house he
himself built so long ago, and hears Solvejg's voice
as she sings her Whitsun-song within.

Then the clouds that have so long veiled the past
begin to roll away, and Peer Gynt, pale as death, recognises the true seat of the "empire," which he has
forgotten, hidden, and sported with so recklessly.
Still he tries to escape, and flees back into the forest.
There, as the grey mists lie sullenly over the desolation left by a mountain fire that has swept over the
forest, he begins at last to see what he might have
been, and what he is. "Falsehood, dreams, and
dead-born knowledge" lie at the base of his pyramid
of life. It rears itself on terraces of lies. Shrinking
from earnestness and from the anguish of repentance
is its shield and device; and the legend peals, as
through the trumpet of doom, "Petrus Gyntus Cæsar
fecit." As he gazes, baby voices, between wailing and
singing, fall upon his ears. "We are thoughts; thou
should'st have thought us; hands and feet thou
should'st have lent us. . . . Aloft we should have
soared as ringing voices; here like grey worsted balls
must we roll and tumble." Withered leaves swept
past by the wind shriek: "We are watchwords.
Thou should'st have planted us! See how torpor has
wretchedly picked at us. The worm it hath eaten
into every lobe of us; and we never could spread like
a crown round the fruit." Sighs are borne through
the air: "We are songs; thou should'st have sung

F

us! A thousand times thou hast smothered and crushed us. In thy heart's mine we have lain and waited, but ne'er were we summoned." The dewdrops dripping from the branches are "tears that were never shed," and the crushed straws "deeds that were never done," which will stand up in judgment against him on the last day.

Peer Gynt has never been himself. Indeed he has not been anyone at all. And this introduces the mysterious button-caster who is to melt his soul in his spoon, as old metal, to coin fresh souls from.

Peer Gynt resents and resists with tooth and claw the idea of this destruction of himself; but the button-caster points out to him that he has never been himself. Inasmuch as the stamp of individuality is entirely effaced, he has really nothing to lose by extinction.

Indignant and incredulous, he first sets about proving that he has always been his true self, as has been his constant boast; but a series of grotesquely or grimly humorous scenes, of a terrible suppressed earnestness, drive him first from the plea that he has been his true self, and then from the plea that he has been even his false and wicked self.

For it appears that if a man has expressed himself *negatively* in strong, characteristic, and original sins, he may be handed over to the proper functionary to be further "developed"—the treatment requiring much sulphur and such like ingredients—till the "positive" likeness is recovered. But "it needs both force and earnestness to sin," and Peer has been too much afraid of committing himself to have qualified himself thus. Not only God's Peer Gynt but the devil's Peer Gynt also is washed out. There has long ceased to be anything decisive or individual in his sins, and since he cannot get an authentic register of them he must go into the melting-spoon. This is what his "hedging" and compromise have brought him to! At last he sees and acquiesces in the justice of the doom. He sees that he is in truth no one. Clasping himself in horror and despair, as if to persuade himself by physical demonstration that there is a Peer Gynt somewhere, he cries :

Is there no one, no one in all the turmoil ! no one in the abyss, no one in heaven !

So unspeakably poor may a soul then go,—back into the grey mists of nothingness. Thou beauteous earth, be not wroth with me that I trod thy grass to no avail. Thou beauteous sun, thou hast squandered thy shining beams on a deserted cottage. There was no man therein to be warmed and attuned. The owner they said was never at home. Beautiful earth and beautiful sun, ye were fools to bear and to shine for my mother. Spirit is chary, and Nature is prodigal ; and 'tis dear to pay with one's life for one's birth. I will up, high up on the steepest rock ; I will once more look on the sun as he rises ; gaze myself weary on the promised land ; then get the snowdrift heaped over me. They may write, " Here lies no one buried," and then, after that, let it go as it may.

Peer Gynt, is ready now to go into the melting-spoon. He has come to know that he is already no

one.   But this very recognition is the first step on a
better way.   As he meets the button-caster again he once
more hears Solvejg's voice, and sees the light in her
cottage.   Then a kind of wild confidence returns.   He
no longer looks for his lost empire; but here at least
he may find his devil's self, and may be saved from
annihilation.   Here he may find the register of sins
which will at least prove him to be some one.   Facing
the anguish and shame of his remorse, for once he
will not "go round," but will break through, be the
way never so hard.   "Like a wild and infinite wail is
this coming in, coming home, coming back!"

Peer Gynt cries out for the tale of his sins from
Solvejg, but as she gropes for him, a blind old
woman, she can only cry, "It is he! it is he!   Now
blessed be God!"   He has made her life a delicious
song.   He has never wronged her.   Blessed is he to
have come once again!   Then his last hope is gone
—unless perchance Solvejg can tell him where his
true self has been.

Peer Gynt.   Lost! if you cannot guess riddles.
Solvejg.   Ask them.
Peer Gynt.   Ask them? ay, verily!   Can you tell me
where Peer Gynt has been since last we met?
Solvejg.   Where he has been?
Peer Gynt.   With the mark of his destiny upon his
brow; e'en as he sprang from God's thought?   Can you
tell me that?   If not, I must wend me home, must sink
into the land of mists.
Solvejg.   Oh, that riddle is easy read.
Peer Gynt.   Then say what you know.   Where have

I been, as myself, whole and true ? Where have I been with God's stamp on my brow ?

Solvejg [*smiling*]. In my faith, in my hope, in my love.

Peer Gynt [*starting back*]. What say you ? Ha ! they are juggling words. To that boy in your heart you yourself are the mother.

Solvejg. His mother I am. But who is his father ? 'Tis he who pardons at the mother's prayer.

Peer Gynt [*as a ray of light from the rising sun falls on him*]. My mother, my spouse, thou innocent woman ! Oh shield me, shield me in thy bosom !

> [*He grips fast hold of her and buries his face in her lap. Long silence as the sun rises.*]

Solvejg [*sings softly*]. Sleep thou, sleep, my darling boy. I will rock thee, I will watch. The boy has sat on his mother's lap. They two have played the whole live-long day. The boy has rested on his mother's breast the whole livelong day. God bless thee, my joy ! The boy has lain so close to my heart the whole livelong day. Now he is so tired. Sleep thou, sleep, my darling boy ! I will rock thee, I will watch.

The *Button-Caster's* voice [*from behind the house*]. We meet at the last crossway, Peer ; and then we shall see—I say no more.

Solvejg [*sings louder as the day strengthens*]. I will rock thee, I will watch. Sleep and dream, my darling.

LECTURE IV.

"EMPEROR AND GALILÆAN," "LOVE'S COMEDY," THE SOCIAL PLAYS.

" BRAND " and " Peer Gynt " were fierce invectives against Norway, but they were welcomed with boundless enthusiasm by the very people they lashed.

It may be doubted whether such a phenomenon has ever been paralleled.   Dramas filled with scathing satire and denunciation of the Norwegians have become as it were the Norwegian national epics.   They have given Norway an exalted sense of national existence and national significance.   They have been read by high and low, are known almost by heart by hundreds of Norwegians, and have enriched the thought, the proverbial wisdom, the imagination, and the language of Norway.   To the wanderer over fell and fiord, they are ever present ; their magic lines so blending with the scenery they describe, that he *sees* them in the snow-field and ice tarn ; and the author of " Peer Gynt " and " Brand " is forgotten and lost— absorbed into the invisible and impersonal genius of the place which has become articulate through his words.

But Ibsen's direct polemic against his people was not yet completed. "Brand" and "Peer Gynt" were

followed by " The Youthful League " (1869), a satire
on the political parties and the political motives of
Norway. This brilliant play is naturally one that ill
bears transplanting, but English readers are in a
position to form their own opinion of its merits in an
English dress, and it is not my purpose to dwell upon
it further than to point out that it is the first of Ibsen's
plays written in that limpid simplicity of current
modern prose which stamps his dialogue in all his
later work with unsurpassed verisimilitude and natural-
ness in the original, and with the inevitable appearance
of baldness in even the best translation.

" The Youthful League" checked Ibsen's rising
popularity. It was received with indignation in his
native land. The philosophical observer may find
much food for reflection in the fact that the people
which not only admired, but positively exulted in
" Brand " and " Peer Gynt," indignantly resented the
" Youthful League." But this too passed away.
My copy bears the date of 1883, and shows that in
that year the work reached its fifth edition.

After writing these three plays, Ibsen at last re-
turned to " Julian the Apostate," and in 1873 the two
dramas, respectively entitled, " Cæsar's Apostasy "
and " The Emperor Julian," but also embraced under
the common title, " Emperor and Galilæan," made
their appearance.

In some respects this is the most ambitious, as well
as the most bulky, of Ibsen's works. It has great
merits, so great, indeed, that it would not be easy to
exaggerate them ; but yet it is almost the only one of

Ibsen's published works that can fairly be called an artistic failure. Critics, I think, are substantially agreed on both these points. The drama gives evidence of a historic sense, the more remarkable since Ibsen was presumably not much of a Greek scholar, and must have depended largely upon translations and secondary sources for his vivid reconstruction of the epoch of Julian. The intolerable atmosphere of suspicion, hypocrisy, and treachery in which Julian passed his youth; his own timid, feverish superstitious, yet attractive character; and the heroic potentialities which never rise into heroism, the talent which never becomes genius, the capacity which never ripens into greatness, and the all-penetrating, all-corroding vanity that are the distinctive characteristics of Julian, are thrown into vivid relief in the first of the twin dramas. In the second we witness the moral and intellectual collapse of a fanatic who lacks inspiration. Julian is a pedant, not a prophet; and his pedantry swallows up his humanity, and dictates actions as revolting and less excusable than the wildest excesses of the Christian fanatics. But he never can adopt the *rôle* of a persecutor with a whole heart. He is ashamed of himself, and is half conscious all along of the hollowness of his own cause. He is engaged in a hopeless struggle against fate, and its hopelessness does not bring out the tragic grandeur of his nature, but saps his force and vitality, and reduces him to insignificance, indecision, and at last to more helpless superstition and crazy arrogance. It is a relief to all, a relief chiefly to himself, when he receives his death

wound, can drop the **weary** struggle, and **can cry,**
"Galilæan! Thou **hast triumphed."**

The whole picture **is drawn with** deep insight both
historical and psychological. But it cannot **be** denied
that the dialogue **often** drags and sometimes over-
stays the climax; **and** that the second **of** the two
dramas has no sufficient development, and no sufficient
interest to sustain **it at** any rate through the first **three**
of its five long acts.

But in spite of all this, there is, perhaps, not one **of**
Ibsen's works which the serious student of the social
plays can less afford **to** ignore than the "Emperor
and Galilæan," **for** here, if anywhere, Ibsen sets forth
his formal creed.

Julian perceives rightly **enough that** the **official**
Christianity of **his** day is hollow **and hypocritical.** It
does not make men spiritual, **but it lays a ban upon**
their earthly **enjoyments, and corrupts and corrodes**
them. It **has quenched** the beauty of **the** old pagan
religion of joy, and has planted in its place a grovelling
religion of superstition, of fear, of bargaining, and of
treachery.

But now that it has once come and has made the
old religion wither, as under a blight, it **is** vain to en-
deavour to recover that old religion **again.** A man
may seek **relief from** the **present by** transporting himself into the **past, but he cannot bring back the** past
into the present and make it **live** again.

When Julian has been **crowning his brow with vine-**
leaves, and seeking the fresh **life of joy and** freedom
that reigned of old, **and has then fallen into a con-**

versation that stirs in his heart thoughts of the passionate earnestness of the early Christian spirit, he cries out that the only real life is to be found in the fire of martyrdom and the crown of thorns ; and as he strikes his hand upon his brow, it falls upon the vine-crown ! Sadly he removes it and gazes on it, then flings it away with the bitter cry, " The new truth is true no more, and the ancient beauty is no longer beautiful ! "

And yet he perpetually strives to recover that ancient beauty, though he feels that it is now hateful. As he rides through the streets in Bacchic triumph with the panther skin thrown over his shoulders and the wild chorus of revellers round him, he tries to imagine that he is restoring ancient beauty ; but no sooner is he alone than he feels the hideous hollowness of the whole thing. Is a band of drunkards and harlots paid to sport in the streets, while the abashed or amused crowd stares in bewilderment, or raises a mercenary shout to please the Emperor,—a shout with no joy, no conviction, no ring in it—is this beautiful?

Beautiful? Nay, he cries out for a bath, a bath for the body and the soul, to wash away the stench of it !

And thus in the war of philosophy against super-stition, of toleration against fanaticism, of beauty and freedom against anxious earnestness, he has changed sides without knowing it. He finds himself engaged in a crusade against luxury, worldliness, and indifference. He strives to lay a new consecration upon men, instead of leading them back into frank and free enjoyment of life. The Galilæan has laid a spell upon the world, and his foe can no more escape it than his followers can.

It is clear enough, then, where Julian is wrong. But what would have been the right? The Christianity he knew was rotten. He could not acquiesce in it. But the true way out of it into something better lay forward, and not backward.

This doctrine is expounded—in a jargon which, it must be confessed, severely tries our patience—by the mystic Maximus. The "Third Kingdom," which is neither that of the Emperor nor that of the Galilæan, and yet is both, which is neither that of the flesh nor that of the spirit, and yet both, neither of beauty nor of truth, and yet both,—the "Third Kingdom," the consummation and harmony of its imperfect predecessors, towards which all rebels against what is have dimly felt their way, which none can describe because none have seen the unborn—this "Third Kingdom" is to be reached *through* the past and the present. Infancy has its beauty, which dies, but is not lost when youth swallows it up. Youth has its beauty, which dies, but is not lost when manhood succeeds it. You cannot go back to *recover* infancy; you must go forward to *preserve* both it and youth transfigured and embraced in manhood.

Thus decisively is the reactionary solution of social and religious problems rejected. When the truths that once inspired men have become mere catchwords, salvation lies in an advance which will recover and reincorporate, while transmuting and transforming, their essential spirit, not in a retreat which will attempt to preserve the perishing or resuscitate the dead formulæ.

And again: the mere fact of any truth being accepted, recognised, formulated, patronised, enforced, and established, itself tends to make it a lie; for it tends to become a convention instead of a formative power, a tradition instead of a conviction, a profession instead of a belief. Hence Julian's established Paganism has all the vices of the established Christianity it superseded, in addition to its own reactionary unreality; and the only vivifying power which his zeal for Paganism really exercises is its purifying influence upon the Christianity which he persecutes. In this, and in this only, he is really effective; for he thus helps to reinvigorate the Christians, and push them forward towards the new truths they had ceased to seek.

Such, I take it, is the meaning of the "Emperor and Galilæan;" and it will be seen how closely it all bears upon the faiths and scepticisms, the advances and reactions of our own day; and what a flood of light it throws upon Ibsen's attitude towards all the problems of modern life in the social plays.

And now my task draws to a close. It was two-fold. I have tried, in the first place, to show some of the grounds upon which I claim for Ibsen the name of poet; and in the next place to point out the clues to the meaning of his later work, which are to be found in his earlier lyrics and dramas.

Let me sum up the results so far obtained. We have seen Ibsen at war with the society in which he lived and with the country that gave him birth, striving to find self-utterance under conditions of life that were cramped and cramping, and traditions that were worn out and sterile. We have seen him turn for relief to an ideal past, but with a growing conviction that the true life must be lived, not in the past, but in the present. We have seen his scorn for sordidness and selfish half-heartedness pour itself out in the lava streams of "Brand" and "Peer Gynt"; and through the storm and wail of these two unapproachable dramas we have heard the passionate demand for self-utterance and self-realisation melt into notes of divine or romantic love;—but with a rebellious protest only half suppressed, and an idealism closely akin to despair. We have seen, gradually emerging and at last reaching clear self-consciousness, the question of questions: "How shall the self-abnegation demanded by society be combined with the self-realisation that is the legitimate demand of the individual, and the salt of society itself? How shall social life and duty be made the support and the expression instead of the charnel house of the free individual life?" The answer has been borne in upon us: "When the ideals of a community are living, the common life will magnify and uplift the life of the individual, and room for self-utterance will be found in self-surrender. When the ideals of a community are dead, and their place has been taken by conventions and lies, then the common life will seek to choke and do to death the life of him who dares to live." We have seen that the escape from these dead and petrified conventional ideals and their resurrection into a higher life lies in advance and not in retreat; that the dead matter must be cut off and cast away, the corpse thrown overboard; and that while he who can wake new life and create a new ideal is the greatest, he too is great who can save us from brooding over the dead, and vainly striving to galvanise or lie it into life.

And thus we have come to understand the meaning and the mission of the " poet of doubt."

Is it not enough after this merely to enumerate the social plays? "The Pillars of Society," "The Doll's House," "Ghosts," "The Enemy of Society," "The Wild Duck," "Rosmersholm," "The Lady from the Sea," "Hedda Gabler."

Well has the " poet of doubt " fulfilled his mission. If he were the mere cynic, with no eye to beauty, and , no belief in nobility of character, who can only see, and only cares to see, what is foul, mean, or repulsive, he would, indeed, have little enough significance for us. But we are speaking of the creator of Lona Hessel and Martha Bernick and her sister, of Dr. Stokman and his wife and daughter and sea-faring friend, of Hedvig Ekdal and Juliane Tesman. For myself I could add many more, but their names might be challenged; and these are enough to vindicate the poet of doubt from the charge of indiscriminate cynicism.

Again: the poet of doubt is not the poet of negation. We have had many apostles of negation, who thought they had found the formula of emancipation in the gospel of reason, and the negation of all

that reason cannot render an account of. How many of
them could stand before Ibsen's judgment-seat, and
come away with the same light-hearted conviction that
everything which they could not demonstrate was mere
superstition? Surely the terrible poet of doubt will not
spare them any more than other believers. There is
many a one besides Fru Alving, who holds that any
feeling for which he cannot give a reason is a mere
" Ghost." Do they know the meaning of their creed?
Let them go with her through the horrors of that night
in which she is called upon to judge whether every
instinct of her nature, and at last whether the very
central purpose and passion of her whole being is a
mere " ghost," and they will, at least, come forth from
that ordeal chastened and sobered, with the glib
confidence in their independence of the past shaken
as perhaps none but Ibsen could shake it, with the
knowledge that they have hardly begun to ask the
questions they thought they had already answered.

Or where can we find anything more searching than
the light thrown in " Rosmersholm " upon the self-
deceptions of a man and woman, who think that, in
their relations one with another, they can ignore the
garnered wisdom and experience of ages, and dismiss
as superficial conventions that have no reference to
them, the resultant beliefs and mandates of society?
Or where can we find a bolder or more virile repre-
sentation at once of the necessity and of the danger of
the rupture with an established moral or religious
order already antiquated, but not yet replaced, than is
embodied in this same " Rosmersholm " ?

Or yet again : if you think you have got the formula of life in a war cry against conventional reticence and lies, and a belief in probing instead of skinning over wounds, go with Gregers Werle on his crusade, and learn how easy it is to think you are setting a man's feet upon the rock of truth, when, in fact, you are calling upon him to act on principles he only respects at second hand, and to profess sentiments he neither feels nor understands.

But where am I to stop ? There is scarcely one of Ibsen's social plays which we can read without being forced to admit that we had somewhere stopped short of the full meaning of our own questions, and accepted an answer that concealed from us the duty, and robbed us of the strength, of deeper questioning.

The poet of doubt has, indeed, fulfilled his mission ! But people say he is "immoral." What do they mean ?

Do they mean that the moral nature is braced by the habitual contemplation of noble and beautiful things ; that it is dwarfed and poisoned by habitual con- templation of horrible, foul, or ignoble things ; that there are some who delight in unwholesome familiarity with what is hateful, and some who are banefully fascinated by it, even while they loathe it ; and that Ibsen is therefore a depressing moral in- fluence ?

If this is what is meant I believe there is truth in it. I doubt not that Ibsen has done, is doing, and will do, moral harm to some of his readers. The same may be said of Thackeray. And—for very different reasons—the same may be said of Goethe, of Carlyle, and of many more. There are minds capable of deriving harm, and perhaps incapable of deriving good, from Ibsen as from these others.

But do people mean more than this when they say that Ibsen is immoral? Do they mean that he makes vice seem attractive, or that he stimulates the imagination to vicious activity? I cannot conceive of such a charge being intended by any man who has read Ibsen; but, unhappily, many use language calculated to convey to those who have not read him, the impression that this is the charge they bring.

Or do they mean that Ibsen's writings tend to confuse moral issues, and therefore to weaken moral restraints? Inasmuch as his works have a terrible solvent power, they may indeed tend to reduce a man to a condition of ethical agnosticism, with all its attendant dangers; but this may be said of all who challenge accepted ideas; and Ibsen is singularly free from the sin of representing a tinsel nobility as genuine, or failing to appreciate the true ore of humanity wherever it is found. In Ibsen, as in Thackeray, the moral *stress* is always true.

But what really lies at the basis of all morality? Is it not the sense of the magnitude of the issues of our thoughts, words, and deeds? He who saps, deadens, or overbears the sense of responsibility, is the really immoral writer. Will any one bring this charge against Ibsen? Who, in our day, has brought home with greater force the significance to others of what we do, what we think, and what we are,

G

than Ibsen? Or who has made us feel the responsibility
sitting closer to us for frivolity in rejecting, or hypocrisy
in accepting, the current code and creeds of society?

But enough of this cheap reproach of immorality.
Let us turn again to the central problem of Ibsen's
social plays. That problem I take to be the relation
of the individual to his social and personal surroundings. Everyone who has given a moment's serious
attention to social facts knows that our personal and
individual life comes to us in and through our "human
environment," and can only express itself fully and
richly when it goes out towards, and in some sense loses
itself in, the life of others. And yet this "life of
others" constantly presents itself to us as a hampering
and dwarfing power, forcing conventions and unver-
acities upon us, and preventing us from ever becoming ourselves. "To be oneself is to slay oneself."
Yes, but, unhappily, there are many other ways of
slaying oneself besides self-realisation; and many
there be that find them.

Now, there is one special case of this problem of
self-surrender and self-realisation so obvious and so
complex, that it cannot fail to have a quite specific
attraction for Ibsen ; and, moreover, conventional
morality and tradition choose persistently to ignore its
true nature. It is the problem of a woman's life when
she marries. Here is a special field for the bold
questioner, whose voice, once heard, may be cursed
or ridiculed, but cannot be forgotten.

If a woman has a life and individuality of her own
before she marries, she is called upon to reconcile

self-realisation with self-surrender in a manner so conspicuous that the blindest cannot fail to see it, when once their attention is called to it. Fatherhood is an incident. Motherhood is an occupation. A man marries and apparently remains himself. When a woman marries she becomes someone else. She changes her name; she changes her home; she changes her occupation; and her new name, her new home, and her new occupation, are determined by her husband and her children. Hence marriage, regarded from the woman's point of view, is the problem of society, focussed and epitomised—the problem of self-realisation in and through self-surrender. The same problem meets us all, men and women, in all the relations of life; but in none is it so obvious and so tangible as it is here. Again, the change in a woman's life when she marries is so great that it may seem to offer her an almost complete escape from conditions that oppress and confine, or haunt, or tease her. She may have at least the appearance of reason on her side if she separates herself from her circumstances and refuses to believe that she is herself the greatest and most important factor in her own life. She may pant for an escape, and may believe that marriage will give her a career. A man may look to marriage for many things, but hardly as in itself opening a career to him. Hence, a woman's temptation to a refined form of mercenary motive in marriage. When she seems to be giving her heart to the man who loves her, she may be in truth bartering herself to him for a position and a career.

Ellida. Now, just listen, Wangel. What is the use of our lying to ourselves—and to each other?

Wangel. Lying, do you say? Is that what we are doing?

Ellida. Yes, that is what we are doing. Or, at any-rate, we are hiding the truth. For the truth, the pure, clean truth, is just this, that you came out there—and bought me.

Wangel. "Bought"! do you say "bought"?

Ellida. Oh! I wasn't an atom better than you were. I agreed to it. I went and sold myself to you.

Wangel. Ellida! have you really the heart to call it so?

Ellida. But what else can I call it? You couldn't endure the void in your house. You were looking about for a new wife.

Wangel. And a new mother for my children, Ellida.

Ellida. Well, perhaps, incidentally, though you hadn't the least idea whether I was fit for the position. You'd only seen me and talked to me once or twice. And you took a fancy to me, and so—

Wangel. Yes! call it whatever you please.

Ellida. And I, on my side—there was I, all helpless and resourceless, and utterly alone. It was so natural for me to fall in—when you came and offered to look after me for all my life.

Ellida feels that she was forced into the transaction which she calls a sale, and her husband calls a marriage. At the very time she is speaking thus to him, Bollette is arranging a transaction, very different in its terms but identical in its nature, with Arnholm. Nora Helmer and Fru Alving presumably drifted into marriage, and promised to surrender themselves before they had come to any consciousness of who and what they were. Not one of them had any real choice, or knew what she was doing. If they had had a choice they would have known that their problem was the problem of life—to find oneself by losing oneself.

I am convinced that it is in this typical significance of marriage, and not in any special interest in the so-called "woman question" as such, that we are to seek the reason of Ibsen's constant recurrence to this theme. Suppress individuality and you have no life; assert it and you have war and chaos. The principle of life is found when we can reconcile the strong utterance of self with self-abnegation; and the necessity of harmonising these two is absolutely forced upon us when we think of marriage. The mere freedom of choice on which Ellida Wangel and Nora Helmer lay such stress is but a condition, not a principle of healthy life. Hedda Gabler neither drifted nor was forced into marriage; but she deliberately and shamelessly paid the flattered and delighted Tesman in the forged coinage of love for opening to her a retreat from the career she had exhausted, and an entry into the best career she could still think of as possible; and we see the result. Without the spirit of self-surrender free choice will never secure self-realisation.

Ibsen may well say that his *forte* is asking questions, not answering them! In this particular matter his questioning began early. And this brings me to the only part of my proper task which I have not yet attempted. There is one of Ibsen's most celebrated and most brilliant metrical dramas that I have not yet so much as mentioned. It is his first work on the conditions of modern society, his first satire, and the first utterance that roused that indignant resentment which has from time to time flamed out against him from that day to this.

I refer to "The Comedy of Love," written in 1862, when Ibsen was still living in Christiania. Its subject is love, courtship, and matrimony, and its hero and heroine are Falk (or Falcon), a young poet and author, and Svanhild, the eldest daughter of the lady with whom he boards.

To us Englishmen there is always something supremely ludicrous in the approved Continental customs and ideas concerning courtship; and Ibsen's relentless satire will be keenly enjoyed by all Englishmen who are fortunate enough to be able to read it in the original. But how can I give those who are not in that happy position any conception of the bevies of fluttering maids and matrons that thrill with delight at the announcement of another engagement, of the excitement which pervades them on the report of a "little misunderstanding" between the newly-engaged couple, of their officious zeal in bringing about a "reconciliation," of their rapturous exclamations when one of them sees Lind kissing Anna's glove, of their vexation and disappointment when the lovers seem tired of being exhibited, of their dismay when the poor harassed "quarry," as his friend calls him,

escapes for a moment; of the clergyman who seizes
every occasion of solemnly discanting on the beauty
and sanctity of domestic joys, and waves his hand towards the eight daughters (out of twelve!) who are
on the scene, with their mother, as living tokens and
pledges thereof; of the sobbing matron, who, with her
handkerchief at her eyes, tenderly dwells upon her
" record" as a match-maker, "seven nieces—and all
of them with boarders"!

And yet, when the curtain falls upon husband and
wife and engaged couples, old and new, kissing each
other two and two, to a grand chorus of the "triumph
of love!" it is difficult to exaggerate the sense of
desolation which swallows up and overwhelms all
amusement, and makes the concluding scene of
" Love's Comedy" one of the saddest pieces of writing
in Isben's works.

Falk has noted from the first with disgust and
scorn how all this "officialism," as it were, marks the
grave of love. As soon as a "lover" is promoted to the
recognised privileges of "my love," the poetry is gone
out of life. Falk looks upon the parson, who braved
public opinion and risked all his future in early life,
for the girl he loved, and who is now the very embodiment of commonplace, conventional, worldly re-
spectability; upon Styver, who once wrote poetry by
the ream, and did not *mend* his pen, but *tuned* it, and
who now treats his *fiancée* with an almost more than
marital indifference; upon his friend Lind who was
intoxicated with love till his engagement was an-
nounced, and now forlornly seeks a moment's escape

from Anna and her friends and aunts,—he looks
upon all these as *corpses*.   Only he and Svanhild who
do not wear their hearts upon their sleeves, who—so
far from parading their love—have never uttered it
even to one another, and like a modern Benedick and
Beatrice are at perpetual war with each other, only
they are alive !

But of course this cannot last.   A misunderstanding forces Falk into a passionate declaration lest he
should lose Svanhild too soon ; but his declaration
has in it the sublimity of masculine selfishness and
arrogance which Ibsen knows so well how to paint.
He is a Falcon, and he must fly against the wind !
He needs Svanhild's support and inspiration to achieve
the height of his poetic calling.   It is her glorious
mission to protect his belief in beauty and love from
" falling " like Adam, during all the spring of her life
and his ; and when she has performed this noble
mission and the leaves begin to fall in autumn, then
the world may claim her, and their ways will part.
The whole relation of course is to be a purely spiritual
one, the idealism of which will not be soiled by the
vulgar cares that make courtship and matrimony the
grave of love !

Svanhild, in answer, reads Falk a lesson under
which he writhes.   But the result of it is to make him
resolve with such intensity as he never put into anything in life before, to win her as his wife, and prove,
up to the hilt, the falsity of the creed which he himself held but now.   For true love need not shrink
from any test and strain of practical life ; and the

vital breath has **deserted** all these spouses and be-
trotheds, not because they have left the ideal for the
real, but because they themselves are of the earth,
earthy. He and Svanhild will **prove that is so.**

His satire becomes fiercer than ever now, but there
is a ringing tone of triumph in it, and when he gives
as his toast amongst all the pairs, married and to be
married, "the late lamented love," he knows that his
own love is victorious.

And so it is. Svanhild is won. She and Falk, side
by side, will wage war against the miserable conventions and pretences of love, and will live the reality.

Then comes Guldstad, the rich middle-aged mer-
chant, and explains to Falk and Svanhild that marriage
is after all a very practical business, involving many
considerations that have not the least connection with
love. You are in love with a *woman*, you marry a
wife ; and a wife has to do and be many things that a
lover, blinded by his love, does not consider. Guldstad himself does not profess to be in love with
Svanhild, but he is convinced that she would make
him an excellent wife, and he can offer her the quiet
stream of a warm and friendly affection and respect,
a sense of the happiness of duty, the peace of home,
and mutual bending of will to will, a tender care to
smooth the path of life for her, a gentle hand to heal
her wounds, strong shoulders to bear, and a strong arm
to support and lift. Can Falk offer her as much?
If so let her take him, and he, Guldstad, who has no
belongings and no claims upon his wealth, will deal
with them as his son and daughter.

Then Guldstad leaves them together. Their love cannot bear the test he has applied to it. *Would* it last in all its triumphant glory, they ask, right on till death? It is so much more than Guldstad has to offer now, but if it should fade and pine, and die down into mere friendship, what a fall were there!

"It will last long," says Falk. But Svanhild answers, "'Long!' 'Long!' Oh wretched word of beggary! How will 'long' serve love's turn? It is death's sentence; mildew on the seed. 'I hold that love has life eternal' shall no more be sung; and the cry shall be, 'A year agone I loved thee!'"

Will it really be more than this? Who shall dare to say? Who shall dare to risk it? Not Svanhild. No! Their love shall know no autumn. It shall remain forever with its beauty undimmed. Their mid-day sun shall know no setting! And Falk accepts her decision. She is his love but must never be his wife. Only by leaving and by loosing her can he win her truly.

So he goes his way. The bevies of ladies eagerly repeat the news, "She's rejected him! she's rejected him!" Her mother presses Guldstad's eligible offer upon her. She asks for a respite "till the leaves are falling;" and as all the "pairs" exult over the discomfiture of the arch-enemy, Falk, who has met his deserts at last from Svanhild, Guldstad offers her his hand, which after an involuntary start, almost a

shudder, she meekly accepts, and the curtain falls upon
" the triumph of love."

What did Ibsen mean by it all? Was the creed of
Falk and Svanhild his own? If so he here fairly
succumbed to the danger indicated in some of his
poems, and fell into the twin vices of sentimentality
and cynicism. For I take it that a man who regards
the passion of love as the richest and most beautiful
thing in life, and who also holds that familiar human
intercourse is essentially and necessarily destructive of
it, is at once a cynic and a sentimentalist. The real
is incapable of being idealised to him, and therefore he
is a cynic ; and his emotional life is essentially un-
real, therefore he is a sentimentalist.

But was this Ibsen's creed? I cannot tell. In any
case " Love's Comedy " was a comparatively early
work, and though it bears a distinct relation to Ibsen's
maturer representations of love and marriage, yet it
does not embody them.

Guldstad's sober but earnest conception of marriage
as a deliberately considered choice, involving manifold
relations not to be entered into lightly, and affecting
every branch of practical life, remains the key-note of
Ibsen's treatment of the subject. And observe that, in
all this, marriage is a type of human relationships in
general. There is nothing specific or unique in it.
Now, the love that draws the opposite sexes one to
the other is something quite unique, but not specifically
human. It pierces right through the animal and vegetable
kingdoms. It is organic and pre-human in its origin.

Remember that profoundly suggestive saying of Peer Gynt's. He had desecrated his relationship to Solvejg, and he says it cannot be patched up again. A *fiddle* can be mended, but a *bell* cannot. A fiddle, with its delicate mechanism, is *constructed*, and when constructed it can be tuned, patched, replaced in pieces, broken and mended. A bell is cast whole in the one molten rush that creates it. It has one note, a note that appeals to something in us deeper than all art, not to be analysed, in one sense not to be developed, to live unchanged—till the bell cracks, and then to be gone for ever.

What we call "falling in love" rings the bell-note in our lives. In its mysterious infra-and-supra-human simplicity it thrills down to the very roots of our organic nature, and yet fills us with the sense of a more than human life. Where it is absent the union of the sexes is unhallowed, and becomes what Ellida calls it, a bargain and a sale; and for men and women who buy and sell in this matter there should be but one name. But marriage is a great deal more besides this "bell-ringing." It is a many-sided and complicated human relationship, and the bell-note, however clear and true it may ring, does not suffice for married life. Details which you may call prosaic if you will enter into the duties of husband and wife. They must be to each other much that partners in business must be, much that servants or other employés must be, much that friends and advisers must be. In a word, their life together must be built up and constructed out of many parts and pieces, to the harmonious fitting of which friendship, good-will, kindly forbearance, and consideration are essential, but which are not secured by "love" in the narrower sense, and may exist without it. And if a man and woman who are "in love," but are not suited to enter into the complicated relations of husband and wife with each other, none the less marry, there is indeed nothing unhallowed in the fact of their union ; but the bell is pretty sure to crack e'er long. And what is there left then ?

Off they go pall mall to the altar, set up a home in the very shrine of happiness, pass a season in an orgie of triumph and faith ; and then comes the day of reckoning, and lo, and behold ! the whole concern is hopelessly bankrupt. The wife's cheek is bankrupt in the bloom of youth, and her heart bankrupt in the flowers of thought. The husband's breast is bankrupt in victorious courage, bankrupt in every glowing spark that was struck of old ; bankrupt, bankrupt is the whole concern ; though they two entered life as a first-class firm of love.

Then does Ibsen teach that because "falling in love," though it be never so many fathom deep, gives no sure promise of wedded happiness, therefore the element of passion should be ignored in marriage? I cannot tell. But this is certain, that he lays the stress of his representations not upon the truth that being "in love" is essential to an ideal marriage, but upon the other truth that it is not enough for an ideal marriage.

He seems always to represent "love," in the romantic sense, in its misleading and delusive character.

Johan Tönnesen is in love, and in consequence he does not "so much as see" Martha Bernick who had been tried and found as true as steel, and who was made to be the companion of his life ; and he marries a girl of whom he knows nothing. Torvald Helmer is in love—note that—in love after many years of married life, still thrilled by the same magnetic influence, still finding in Nora's society the same unreasoning and unanalysable delight which first drew him to her. And therefore he thinks himself a model husband, when really his relations with his wife have never risen above mere organic attraction, and have never been human at all. Rebekka West is in love, and her love leads her into depths of treachery and cruelty that make "Rosmersholm" one of the most appalling of Ibsen's dramas ; and Rosmer himself is in love, and his love drives him to leap with Rebekka into the dark pool below the foss. And lastly, Ellida is in love, and in her the untamed, pre-human nature of love, as Ibsen conceives it, comes out in its full significance. Like the heaving of the sea to the moon, like the craving of the stranded mermaid for the deep ocean, unreasoning, and not to be reasoned with, dark and deep and wild, this elemental drift and up-heaval of our nature must be tamed and mastered, that our relations, one with another, may be sober, well-considered, and human.

And is this all? Does Ibsen know that in considering marriage in this sober, human, rational style, he is leaving out the specific element in it, and dealing with it only as typical of all human relationships?

Does he ignore the truth that in the ideal marriage the bell-note rings from first to last, and that all else is dominated and glorified by it? Does he know that it is only that "love" which has its roots far down beneath our humanity that can raise marriage, as such, into a truly human relationship? I will not answer for him. There are indications, deep rather than numerous, especially in "The Doll's House" and in "The Lady from the Sea," that he knows all this as well as any of us. But at any rate he does not choose to dwell upon it. He chooses to dwell upon marriage under its other aspects. And can we afford to be ungrateful to him? How many marriages are there that, tried by the ideal standard, will not be found wanting? They may be few or many, but at least they are something less than all. And what of the others? The bell is cracked. Are husband and wife simply to sit down and say that life is a failure, or at least that they can be nothing to each other now? Surely they may be much. The tenderness of considerate friendship, and the mutual helpfulness of loyal partnership are not love, but in their measure they are beautiful and life-giving; neither is love a substitute for them, even where love is. That the bell is sound, or that the bell is cracked, is an equally foolish reason for not mending the broken fiddle, or tuning its neglected strings.

With respect to marriage, then, I do not find in Ibsen the highest truth insisted on with any distinctness or directness. He even leaves me in doubt whether he is not profoundly mistaken in his teaching;

but he works out some aspects of the problem with a piercing insight and a relentless truth, for which I have no words but those of grateful admiration. If I can find the husband and wife who show me that they have read and understood "The Doll's House," "Rosmersholm," and "The Lady from the Sea," but that they had nothing to learn from them, then I will lay down Ibsen, and ask leave to sit at their feet. But I do not expect that this will be either to-day or to-morrow.

In conclusion, then, the strength and the weakness of Ibsen's much discussed treatment of marriage lies in the fact that he does not deal with it as marriage at all, but as the most striking instance of the ever recurrent problem of social life, the problem that we may hide in other cases, but must face here, the problem of combining freedom with permanence and loyalty, of combining self-surrender with self-realisation.

THE END.

Printed by Cowan & Co., Limited, Perth.